"Shadow of the Moon"

M/M Wolf Shifter Paranormal Romance

Further Chronicles of Lycanthia Volume 1

Apollo Surge

© 2020
Apollo Surge

This book is intended for Adults (ages 18+) only. The contents may be offensive to some readers. It may contain graphic language, explicit sexual content, and adult situations. May contain scenes of unprotected sex. Please do not read this book if you are offended by content as mentioned above or if you are under the age of 18. Please educate yourself on safe sex practices before making potentially life-changing decisions about sex in real life.

This story is a work of fiction. Names, characters, businesses, places, events and incidents are the products of the author's imagination or used in a fictitious manner and are not to be construed as real. Any resemblance to actual persons, living or dead, or actual events is purely coincidental. Products or brand names mentioned are trademarks of their respective holders or companies. The cover uses licensed images and are shown for illustrative purposes only. Any person(s) that may be depicted on the cover are simply models.

Edition v1.00 (2020.09.11) apollo@apollosurge.com

Special thanks to the following volunteer readers who helped with proofreading: RB, N. Watson, Big Kidd, and those who assisted but wished to be anonymous. Thank you so much for your support.

Prologue

The kingdom of Lycanthia is a hidden jewel. A small country nestled in the bosom of Europe, it resembles a place from a fairy tales. Its buildings are quaint, its people are kind, and the sun always shines upon the beautiful landscape. Few people have heard of it, but for those who live there and for those who have experienced the rare sights of the place, they know it is special.

It is also a place of mystery. Lycanthia was founded a long time ago as a sanctuary for werewolves, a place where they could be safe from those that hunted them, as the story goes anyway. As generations passed more people came to Lycanthia, pureblood humans, and the population became mixed. Rumors and whispers drifted through the shadows of the world, tempting people with the truth. Some came to hunt for magical relics, some came to sate their curiosity, while others came to hunt these 'monsters'.

Due to her father's carelessness, Queen Freya declared that the wolves should remain secret. She ordered them to hide their identity so that they should never be discovered, and thus never be harmed. But her fear and paranoia meant that the wolves lost something special about themselves. They lost their pack. Her son, Eric von Arnheim, grew up to be a strong and mighty wolf. When he came of age and learned of the true history of his country and his people, he was filled with conflict. While he respected his regal mother, he couldn't help but disagree with her. It was wrong for them all to be so lonely, to be defined by their fear.

Wolves should never be afraid of anything.

With his consort by his side, the human man Shane (their romance was an open secret among the people of Lycanthia, although their wedding had remained a private affair), Eric set about changing the rules. He managed to convince the Queen that she had been wrong to isolate the wolves. Together they brought the wolves back together and ran as a pack once again.

The catalyst for this was the birth of a son, a new prince, Boris von Arnheim, heir to the throne and the new Prince of the Wolves.

Eric and Shane ushered in a new era of peace and compassion; a time where people didn't have to look over their shoulder in paranoia or worry about threats to their lives.

But there are still people out there who wonder about the mysteries that Lycanthia holds. There are still those who know more than they should.

And they're coming.

Chapter One

"Yes, keep going, chase it down!" Freya called in a shrill voice. Boris felt the wind whip against his body. The air was alive with the scent of the hunt. His prey galloped ahead of him, the majestic deer thumped its hooves, sending up small explosions of dirt from the ground as it hurtled away. Boris' heart beat as only a hunter's heart could beat; filled with a lust and hunger for blood, a primal excitement as he indulged his most savage and natural desires. He could almost taste the hide of the deer in his mouth and began to salivate.

His grandmother's voice was distant and vague to him, but that was always the way when he shifted into a wolf. The human qualities grew vaguer, as though they were a part of another world, or a dream...although the less said about dreams the better. Becoming a wolf was a great freedom and Boris felt blessed that he should be able to transform into a wolf. Not everyone could, like his father Shane. This had come to quite a shock when Boris was younger. He just assumed that everyone could do it.

But then, there were plenty of things that had come as a shock to him. He was the only person he knew that had two fathers. Eric was the king and Shane was his, well, technically he was a Queen, but he didn't like being called that. He preferred the term consort. His mother lived far away in another country, although she wasn't really his mother, people just believed that. He had been carried by Shane in what was said to be a miracle. To Boris, it was just normal. And so was being a wolf. There was nothing more natural to him than shifting into the form of a savage beast and running through the world. The call of the wild sang loudly in his mind, becoming a chorus that could not be silenced. It was alluring and tempting, and it always made him uncomfortable when he had to remain human for a long time, as though he was wearing an itchy outfit that was a size too small. As far as he was concerned, he was a wolf first and a human second.

His paws tore up grass as he sprinted toward his prey. Every lithe sinew in his body was primed for the hunt. His muscles screamed out, his claws were bared and his beady golden eyes were narrowed, focused on nothing but his prey. The landscape around him seemed to blur in a watercolor blend of greens and browns. His white fur stood out starkly, and fear was etched into the deer's face as he knew what was coming for him. Inside Boris' mind it was as though something bestial had taken over. The wolf part of him overwhelmed the human sensibilities and he let go of everything that tied him to the human world. He growled and snarled as he closed the distance to his prey and then made the final leap. The deer whimpered and yelped as it tried to get away, but its long, loping legs simply weren't fast enough.

Boris pounced with outstretched limbs, his claws dug into the deer's hide, sinking into the flesh. Deep gash marks were made and the deer collapsed to the ground, thrashing around with its antlers, in agony. If one of those sharp tips had found a vulnerable part on Boris' body he would have been done for. Boris dodged this way and that to avoid them. It was difficult to predict where the antlers were going to strike since the deer was moving by instinct, so Boris had to be careful as he made his move and nipped in, sinking his teeth into the deer's neck. He felt the sweet, warm flow of crimson nectar flood his mouth and the thrashing of the deer lasted only moments more, until it settled into the calm tranquility of death.

Boris stepped back and threw his head to the sky and let out an almighty howl to alert the world of a successful hunt. Deep in the recesses of the forest there came the echo of another howl, as another wolf answered his call.

This pleased him.

He looked down at his handiwork and tore a chunk of meat away from the deer, taking his right as the victor of the hunt. There was no meat more delicious than that which had been hunted, he thought. His fur was flecked with blood and then he padded away to a nearby babbling brook. The water was clear and he could see his reflection. The golden eyes looked back at him; the blood-stained face was shadowed in crimson. Even his teeth were stained and as he looked at himself, he knew it was easy to understand why some saw the wolves as monsters.

But he wasn't a monster, this was just his nature.

He bowed his head and lapped up the fresh, cool water. It trickled down his throat and lingered on his fur, washing away the remnants of the hunt.

"You did well today Boris," Freya said as she came up behind him. Her hair was as white as his fur, and her skin was so pale it was almost translucent. She walked with a cane now, a gnarled stick that had been carved from a branch of the oldest tree in the forests of Lycanthia. She moved quickly for a woman of her age, although this was because she was fueled by the blood of wolves. Boris continued to drink from the stream until he had had his fill and then turned to face his grandmother. He looked up at her through his beady eyes and then, reluctantly, he embraced the human part of himself that lingered in his mind.

Closing his eyes, he breathed deeply and felt it come unto him, and then he felt his body change. The fur receded into his flesh; the shape of his body changed. It was exquisite agony, but it was a pain he had quickly gotten used to.

Then, there stood a man where moments ago there had been a wolf. He was a handsome man too. Still young, taking his first steps into manhood, Boris had a blending of the best features of his parents. He had the broad shoulders and muscular physique of his father, as well as the shock of auburn hair that was thick and lustrous. From Shane he had inherited soft and sensual lips, and sapphire almond shaped eyes that looked like two jewels.

"Thank you, grandmother, but please do not say it's time to return to the castle yet. I'm not ready," Boris said.

Freya's thin lips curled into a small smile. "You are never ready," she said.

"I have been preparing for this all my life and it's even better than I imagined! I can't believe that is has been denied me all these years."

"That is simply the nature of things," Freya replied enigmatically. She often replied like this and it frustrated Boris.

"But why? Why do we only begin to shift when we turn eighteen? It seems strange that we lose so much of our lives before we can even become wolves."

"It is a nature of the original enchantment," Freya said. "And it is a good thing; your body needs to grow strong enough to handle the act of shifting. It takes a great toll on our hearts, and one day you will find that it is difficult to shift again."

"Is that why you don't shift as often as you used to?"

"Indeed, it is," Freya said sadly. "But it is better to not dwell on the things we cannot do. You are showing great progress in the hunt, but I can tell you missed an opportunity to strike. You let the deer run free for longer than it should have.

"I know. I was enjoying myself too much. I didn't want it to end."

Freya's head dipped as she shook her head. Her hands were clasped on her cane, using it to steady herself. "And in doing so you prolonged its suffering. You must have respect for the world around you Boris. We are a part of nature and there is a balance that must be respected. Yes, we can hunt the deer and the other prey in the forest, but we must not toy with them or treat them cruelly. Furthermore, you should always strike when you see the opportunity. As wolves we are swift and deadly. That is our nature, our instinct-"

"And we should never betray our instincts," Boris said sullenly, finishing off her sentence for her. It was one of the lessons Freya had hammered home to him since a young age. His reaction seemed to amuse Freya as she continued.

"Indeed, but it is not something you should be casual about. By not taking the opportunity when it was presented to you, you gave the deer a chance to escape. There may come a time when you are chasing something more powerful than a deer, something that is not afraid of fighting back, and if you give them a chance you may end up paying the ultimate price. But that is not to say you did not do well. You are still young, yet you are showing remarkable progress.

Your fathers will be proud. Now, let us return home. I think we have spent enough time out here today."

Boris hung his head. "Are you sure? Can't we stay out here a little longer? It's such a nice day and the castle is so boring. I'd like to be a wolf for a little longer. I just want to feel the wind in my hair again, to run free. I can't do that in the castle. It's so annoying. All through my childhood my fathers told me I was special and I was going to be different from most people, but that I would have to wait. So, I was good, and I waited and waited. Now that I'm actually able to shift, I keep being told that I have to stop. It doesn't feel right. When I'm human, all I can think about is becoming a wolf again..." he looked longingly at the forest, turning his gaze away from the tall tower of the castle that peeked over the woods.

Freya moved closer to him and placed her hand on his shoulder. Her fingers were delicate and slender.

"I know it can be challenging to live in a world like this and to feel like your natural instincts have to be curbed, but it is part of our nature. It will get easier, and you will have plenty of opportunities to explore both aspects of your soul. Life is all about balance Boris. Just as there is a balance in nature," she gestured with a hand to the forest, and then pointed to his heart, "there is a balance inside you as well. You should never favor one part of yourself over the other."

Boris nodded. It was something she had told him before, and yet he still couldn't quite grasp it. Being human was ordinary and, well, boring. When he was a wolf, he felt alive, as did the world. There was a vibrancy and a vividness to everything around him that was intoxicating. It was as though new things were open to him, and then subsequently closed off when he turned back into a human. It was all very well and good for Freya to say that he had to get used to it because that was the way the world worked, but that didn't satisfy Boris. He wanted to know *why* things worked that way. Who made the rules? There was so much that seemed unfair, and he didn't know where to start righting the wrongs.

***

They made the short walk back to the castle. Freya didn't say much, enjoying the peace of nature. She walked slower than Boris would have liked, but she was old and Boris had to respect that. Sometimes though he thought she did it deliberately to teach him patience. The castle was busy with bustling people as usual, and they all greeted him with a smile. They would be his subjects one day, although in truth Boris didn't have much interest in being a King. Some of them gave a different smile, and he recognized these as fellow wolves. It always gave him a thrill to see them in broad daylight as it made him feel more validated. They did gather as a pack, but it was still a secret thing, held under the shadow of the moon, away from the city. Boris would love one day to be able to shift in front of other people and not have to worry about the consequences. Everyone had always told him he had to be careful even though they hadn't been able to describe what he should be careful of. As far as he knew nobody declared war on Lycanthia and nobody had come to hunt them.

As he walked through the castle pretty girls blushed and smiled shyly at him. He returned their expressions with politeness, but quickly moved away. Freya noticed this.

"Have you given any thought to your future?" she asked.

12

"Much thought, but to which aspect of my future are you referring?"

"I think you know which aspect," Freya said with a knowing smile. Boris clenched his jaw and felt uneasy tension settling in the pit of his stomach.

"I don't think I have any interest in that, in men or women. Romance seems like a waste of time. What good does it do anyone?"

"I don't think Eric and Shane would like to hear that. Romance has been the defining quality of their lives. I know all they want for you is that you find someone who makes you as happy as they make each other."

Boris made a snorting sound. "I make myself happy. I don't see why I should bother with anyone else when they're only going to take time away from the things I enjoy. Other people only make you obligated to them, and I'd rather not deal with that," he said haughtily. But, deep inside, his heart trembled as he thought of the dream that plagued him, a dream that he had not shared with anyone.

"You sound like me when I was your age. I didn't think I needed anyone. Marriage was just something I had to do to ensure that the country was strong and safe, and to provide an heir. That is what life is about. We are all links in a chain, and it is our duty to see that the chain does not break. Your grandfather on the other hand fell in love with me as soon as he saw me. He made his feelings known, and I found him to be the most agreeable of my suitors." A vague smile crept across her face as she remembered the heat and passion of her youth. "And it was flattering to have him fawning over me. It didn't take long for him to win me over, although I made sure he didn't know exactly how quickly it took. History has a way of repeating itself so I'm sure that the same will happen to you too."

"I wouldn't hold out hope," Boris said, perhaps a little more tersely than he should have, but Freya didn't pay any attention to his tone. "I wish I could have known grandfather better," Boris added.

"As do I. I thought that at some point I would get used to life without him, but it is a longer process than I imagined. There are still times when I wake up in the middle of the night and...I'm sorry Boris. I know you don't want to hear about the problems of an old, foolish woman."

"It's okay grandmother. I don't mind."

"You're a good boy, and I know you're going to have a good life too. Just have some common sense and trust your instincts. They will lead you far."

***

Freya left to go to her chambers, while Boris went into the throne room where Eric and Shane were sitting together, hands clasped. By just looking at them it was clear they were in love. There was a radiant glow about them, and Boris wondered how they made it look so easy. It was as though the two of them were of one heart, completing each other. When they saw Boris, they smiled widely. The throne room had been busy during the day, with the people of Lycanthia coming to speak to their monarch to air their concerns and ask for help. But now the throne room was being emptied. The King and his consort were beginning to relax. Boris walked up to them and they spoke in low tones, so that their conversation would not be heard by anyone else.

"How was your time in the forest?" Shane asked.

"It was wonderful, although all too short," Boris said. "I wish I could spend more time out there."

"I'm glad you're getting on well with your grandmother. She knows a lot." Eric replied.

"She is very wise, but there is still much I do not understand."

"Unfortunately, that will never change," Eric said with a wry smile. "The world is a place of mystery and we will never get the answers to the questions we seek."

Boris knew better than to argue with his parents in this instance. He was tired and didn't have the energy, and there was already something else he wanted to know.

"When is the next gathering father?" he asked, turning to Eric.

"Tomorrow night I believe. But first there is something we must talk to you about. When I was your age, I had to have the same conversation with my parents, and now-"

Boris interrupted him as politely as he could. "I'm sorry, but do you think we could do that a little later? I spent a lot of energy in the woods and I'm tired now. I'd rather rest. I'm still getting used to…everything," he said. Shane and Eric glanced at each other. They looked a little disappointed. Boris put on a false expression to exaggerate his tiredness, for in truth he knew what they were going to talk about and he didn't have the patience for it right now. So often was he forced to face the future, and sometimes he just wanted to focus on the present. Without waiting for them to answer, Boris spun on his heels and strode away to his chambers where he pulled off his clothes and rested in bed. He stared up at the ceiling and looked at his body, wishing that he could just go outside and curl up in the sun, sleeping as a wolf.

When he closed his eyes, he tried to calm his mind, even though fear lined his thoughts. Every time he slept there was always fear about the dream returning. It didn't come every time he slept, but it was always on his mind. He wasn't lying about being tired though. Being a wolf did take a lot out of him and he could understand why it wasn't possible for children or older people to shift as much as he thought should be possible. There were so many rules and things he didn't understand. He was quite certain he had only begun to scrape the surface of what was possible. There were so many mysteries yet to be discovered, and he didn't care what Eric said; there were always answers to questions if one looked hard enough, and Boris wasn't going to be satisfied until he uncovered all the mysteries of his people and his country.

***

Boris awoke in a field. The moon hung in the sky, but it was not its usual shining silver color. It was blood red. His heart filled with fear and his face was ashen. The ground was hard and cold. The trees were naked, shorn of their leaves and danger simmered around him. He was afraid to turn his gaze for he knew what awaited him. It was always the same thing that awaited him in this dream, and no matter how hard he tried to avoid the landscape, it was as though his body moved by itself. He moaned as he looked around at all the wolves chained to the world. Some of them were still alive and howled for mercy, but he was unable to free them. Although he was not chained there was something else holding him back, something preventing him from moving. All he could do was watch as the wolves writhed in pain.

And then a shadow loomed over him. A calm washed over him, like a tide washed over a beach. Boris looked up and saw the man, tall and handsome, a man who seemed to make everything better. He caressed Boris' cheek and Boris' heart melted. Yes, everything would be okay. Everything…

As Boris gazed up at this mystery man, he lost sight of the rest of the world. The howls of the wolves grew fainter and blood red moon receded into the night. There was only this man, only the deep desire and longing that pulled Boris toward him.

Chapter Two

"How are you finding life in Lycanthia Tristan?" Emilia asked as she served another helping of the thick and nutritious stew. Tristan smiled in thanks.

"It's a lovely place. Byron told me many stories about the place, but seeing it is another matter entirely. I am honored to be here," Tristan replied. The man was young, around eighteen. He had a lean figure, but it was muscular. Byron had taught him to train his mind and be disciplined with how he used his body. The lessons had been hard, but they had also been successful.

Tristan had been used to traveling around the country, investigating all kinds of ancient sites. Byron had shown him the world and taught him so much. His home had been a small cottage on a hill in England where most of the space had been taken up by books and Byron's strange experiments. Tristan had seen a lot of strange things in his time so there wasn't much that could surprise him. But now he was sitting in a strange home, in a strange country. Byron was basically his adoptive father and this was his new family, although Tristan didn't feel a connection with them. Emilia seemed nice. She was soft and caring like a mother should be and her doting nature reminded him of his own. Peter was quiet and looked at Tristan curiously, but always darted his eyes away when Tristan met his gaze.

The house was small, quaint, and reminded him of the cottage at home, although it was strange to not be surrounded by the musty smell of books or the different concoctions that Byron mixed. The food was lovely, and Tristan couldn't help but feel uneasy. For such a long time it had just been him and Byron, and while Byron had always hinted at a larger mission in play, it had always seemed like something that would never come to pass. Tristan had liked his life. It was reliable and routine, but now all that had been shattered thanks to Byron's purpose.

"Thank you for having me for dinner," Tristan added, being polite.

"You're quite welcome. It's good for Peter to have a friend. Byron, I have to say I was surprised to hear from you after so long. It's something of a miracle. I was beginning to worry that you would never return," Emilia said. Byron leaned back in a chair that was positioned at the head of the table. He dabbed a napkin around his mouth and sighed happily as he welcomed more stew into his bowl.

"Yes, well, I always did intend to return eventually, and after your letter the timing just seemed right. I never did agree with the rules that Queen Freya laid down for us. But now that things have changed for the better...well, how could I resist?"

Emilia looked a little warily toward Tristan, as did Peter.

"Are you sure it's fine to talk about...*things*," Emilia said.

Byron chuckled. "Oh yes, it's perfectly fine. Tristan knows all about everything, as did his parents before him. Secrecy was never the way to go about our lives and I'm glad that Freya saw the error of her ways, and that her son has managed to make the changes persist over the duration of his reign. No, there's no need to keep everything so hidden. Tristan has been a devoted servant to me and is very bright. I have never met anyone with his instincts before," Byron said, looking with pride at the only pureblooded human at the table.

Tristan smiled and swelled at the praise from Byron, but his heart was filled with mixed feelings as Byron had mentioned his parents as well. Tristan was still angry and bitter about the way that they had been plucked from the world. He had been young, just a boy, with so many things that he was yet to understand. His parents were under the employ of Byron, performing tasks for him and accompanying him on his research missions. And then, one day, they had gotten too nosey for their own good. They had delved into things that shouldn't have concerned them and suffered the consequences. One of Byron's experiments had gone awry because of their interference and it had cost them their lives. They had left Tristan alone, and he would never forgive them for it.

Since then, Byron had raised Tristan as his own child and taught him everything he needed to know about life, including the supernatural mysteries that underpinned the world. He would never forget the day that Byron had revealed to him his true nature. Tristan had always known that something was different. There were nights when the moon was high that he had heard a wolf howl, and there were always whispers from his parents, secret things that fell into silence whenever Tristan entered the room. He heard strange noises coming from the parts of the house where he wasn't supposed to go, and his mind conjured up various different images as to what might be happening.

And then, after his parents died Byron sat down and told him everything. Tristan wasn't sure whether to believe it at first, but then Byron rose and shifted into a lean, black wolf. The beady eyes stared at him, the sharp teeth promised death, but Tristan had felt oddly calm in the presence of the beast. Somehow, he knew that Byron would never hurt him, and he was more intrigued than anything. Byron had smirked when he shifted back into a man and seemed pleased with Tristan's reactions. Since then they had explored the world and tried to find answers to the mysteries of life. Tristan had often expressed a desire to become a wolf himself.

"That is not something you should play around with," Byron had warned him, "the spells of such a desire are not an easy thing to master. There is only one artifact I know of that can provoke such a change, and its results are not easily predicted. Besides, the Chalice of Sinterbaum has been long lost. I do not even know if it exists any longer," he said. Tristan was left feeling disappointed. There were elixirs and decoctions that could grant Tristan abilities close to those of the wolves; with heightened senses and strength and agility, but he could never change from his human form, could never shed his flesh in the way that Byron could and it made him feel incomplete.

One day though, one day Tristan would turn into a wolf. That was his goal, his secret ambition that he held close to his breast even though Byron said that it was impossible.

And now he was in the home of the wolves, Lycanthia, that special country that had been set aside for the supernatural creatures. Byron had often waxed lyrical about the beauty of his homeland and upon Tristan's arrival, the young man had seen for himself that Byron had not been exaggerating. Tristan had seen many different places in his young life, but few had touched his heart as readily as Lycanthia had. Even just walking through the town square had been a joy. It was like something out of a storybook, although he had to get used to keep his master's secret.

But at the dinner table with Byron's family he could speak freely about the wolves, and they seemed relieved to speak freely with him.

Emilia sighed with relief as she filled her bowl and settled into her chair.

"It is a great relief to see that things have changed. There was a point that I thought Peter would have to go through all his life without ever seeing another wolf. You don't know what it was like before Eric took charge and changed the rules. I felt like a monster. Every time I went outside, I had to worry that someone was going to see me. It's never a good thing to be ruled by fear," she said.

"No indeed, but now the wolves are free again," Byron said.

"I'm glad you're back," Emilia said, smiling weakly at Byron. "I never wanted you to go, and when Daniel died, well…it's good to have family close at hand."

"Yes, it is. Frankly I'm sorry that I stayed away for so long. Being back here reminds me that there is no greater place than home. The world has many wonders to behold, but none of them can quite touch the heart like stepping upon familiar territory can."

"Will you be staying here for long?" Emilia asked. Tristan could sense the fear in her voice.

"For as long as I'm able. I know that Tristan has wanted to see Lycanthia for a long time and I would hate to deprive him of the experience."

"There are still some rules though," Emilia said quickly. "He can't come to the gathering."

Byron sighed. Tristan looked down at his stew. He knew such a thing wouldn't have been possible. There were still some divisions that existed between the wolves and the humans. "Such a thing was expected and is still a shame. But I can understand given what has happened in our past. The last thing we want is to have threats to Lycanthia again. As long as wolves are free to socialize with each other and express our true natures we should be thankful. That is, after all, what this country was founded upon."

Emilia looked relieved. "It is indeed, and in time you'll see that Eric has done great things with the country. He's learned the best lessons from his mother and father."

"I'm sure he has, and Pontus too no doubt," Byron said, examining his fingernails.

"Well yes, although Pontus died some years ago now," Emilia looked sorrowful. "The more time passes the more we have to say goodbye to people we once knew. It seems as though we lose more and more people every year," she said.

"It's only an illusion," Byron replied in a confident, brusque manner, "because we also welcome new people in the world as well. The future is built on the shoulders of the young men and women that are growing before our eyes. I'm sure that Peter is a man you can be proud of and will be a fine wolf too," Byron said. Tristan looked over at Peter, who seemed intent on staring at his dinner.

"Oh, he is, and he's providing a valuable service to the town as well. He goes out there every day, hunting for fish, just like his father did," Emilia beamed, taking pride in the humble trade. Peter smiled with embarrassment. Privately, Tristan couldn't think of anything worse than having to go out on the water and catch fish day in day out, being surrounded by the smell of brine, but he kept his thoughts to himself.

"What a wonderful thing!" Byron clapped his hands together.

***

After that, Byron and Emilia talked about the past and other family members that had died. Tristan's mind wandered as it wasn't his family. He waited patiently for the evening to be over when they could retreat to the small hermitage that Byron had arranged for accommodation. They were used to their privacy and so didn't want to burden Emilia with their presence. As they walked away from the house Tristan gazed up at the tall tower of the castle. It loomed over the city impressively, and Byron caught Tristan looking at it.

"Ah, so you're intrigued by the royal family?" Byron asked with a twinkle in his eyes. "I can't blame you really, it is quite a sight. I used to stare up at the castle myself on more than one occasion when I was younger. It's quite open to the general public, but I find there is always something strange about walking through their home. It's quite galling to look at the extravagance and know that no matter how much you work or how hard you try, you will never reach their standards. And why? All because of their bloodline. The world is built on inequality Tristan, it's a grim truth that we all must accept."

Tristan knew that truth well. It was something he had to live with every day, after all.

"That's a bit like you being able to shift into a wolf while I can't, wouldn't you say?" Tristan said with a teasing smile. Byron chuckled to himself and nodded.

"You've caught me out there. I suppose you're right Tristan; that was very quick. The difference is, of course, that there are more wolves than there are kings, and the kings have more power. It's quite often the case that those in power do not deserve it and cannot make the right decisions. Lycanthia is a wonderful place in many respects, but in the manner of its ruling it is backwards. Power should be something given to the wisest and most intelligent people, not to the ones who are born into a certain position. That was one of the reasons why I left in the first place. I knew that I could never be a king here, so I thought I'd seek my fortune elsewhere."

"Has anything changed now?"

Byron had a thoughtful look on his face. "I'm not sure. But there is a new prince, who will in time become a king. The wise man can never become a king, but he can become the next best thing."

"Which is?"

"The king's advisor," Byron said with a wry smile. "There may be an opportunity to influence the future of Lycanthia in a positive way after all. It would never have been possible with Freya. She was always too strong-minded and never listened to anyone's opinions other than her own. But her grandchild? Yes…that may work. We shall see. I shall have to investigate what this prince is like at one of the gatherings."

"Should you be interfering in affairs like this? I thought you wanted to come back and visit, not to get a position in the royal court."

Byron sucked in breath and continued to stride forward through the dark streets. He was a tall man, and despite his slender frame he cut an impressive figure. Tristan had to hurry to remain beside him.

"I have always longed to have some influence over the matters of the country. I was but a young wolf when Freya decided that we should isolate ourselves in the name of protection. I didn't agree with her then and I would like to do all I can to prevent that from ever happening."

"What was the country like back then?"

Byron waved a hand dismissively. "Much like it is today, except there were more wolves and there was more trust in other people. The gates of Lycanthia were open to anyone who was intrigued by the promise of the country. There were some men who wanted to learn about the wolves, and some men who wanted to rob us. The King was old and senile. He was far too compassionate with those who came to Lycanthia and he trusted far too many people. It ended up costing him his life. He was a fool, but then Freya was just as much as a fool for going in the opposite direction. There is no telling how much progress we lost as a race because of her actions. She cut the tethers that bound us and we were cast into an abyss. We couldn't work together any longer, nor did we have access to the relics of the past. With that one act she had taken away everything that I held dear in my life. I was forced to leave and continue my studies. And the relics are all located there," Byron twisted his body around and thrust a thin finger toward the castle. "There is a chance for us to learn so much while we are here, and we cannot pass up the opportunity."

"What about Emilia and Peter? Are they going to help us?"

Byron made a snorting sound. "I shouldn't think so. Emilia never had the mind for this sort of thing. She just likes the company. As for Peter, well he seems to have too much of his father in him. Imagine being proud of doing something simple like fishing? It's a job that anyone could do. Wolves are meant for something better than that."

Tristan nodded in agreement. Wolves were the superior race and there was no denying it. They were faster, stronger, and their senses were far more acute than those of normal humans. They were almost like gods walking among men, and they deserved to be treated as such. Tristan made note of this chalice that Byron had mentioned. It may well have been lost to time, but there may have been something similar in existence, and if there was it was likely to be in the castle. If so, that would be the key to him becoming a wolf, and there was nothing he wanted more in life.

Chapter Three

Boris awoke the following day feeling forlorn. He sat on the edge of his bed and held his head in his hands. The dream, the nightmare had been in his mind for a long time. The fact that it repeated itself was worrying. Yet he hadn't told anyone about it, but the more it came to him the more he worried. But who could he tell? It seemed silly that he should be so worried by a simple dream, and yet he couldn't forget the images he saw; the wolves seemed in pain, and he was the only one free. And who was that man? Why was he standing above Boris? It didn't make any sense.

He tried to vanquish these thoughts from his mind as he got dressed and prepared to go and see his parents. He had delayed the inevitable for too long already. They were going to talk to him about getting married and having an heir. His responsibilities had been made clear to him from a young age, but instead of being reassuring they had only acted like a weight around Boris' neck. Instead of being free to pursue his own dreams and ambitions he had to play the role that had been written for him, and such a thing felt oppressive and suffocating. Only when he was a wolf, was he truly given freedom.

His parents had risen and were in their chambers. Boris knocked on the door and opened it, finding them in an embrace beside the window. The morning sun poured in and cast them in a golden light. They looked up and welcomed their son in.

"Morning Boris," Shane said. Eric offered Shane some fruit, which Boris took.

"Your father and I have been talking. We know it's a difficult time for you and we don't want to put any pressure on you," Shane said. "We went through a similar thing when we were your age. Eric didn't want anything to do with this subject either, but it is something that's important. Unfortunately, your life has never been your own. You are beholden to the people of Lycanthia, and that includes all the wolves. There has been much change over the course of your life. Eric has overseen a complete transformation of the wolf pack, and we'd like to see that continue. You can carry on his good work."

"And to do this I need to be married?" Boris asked tersely. Shane glanced at Eric, who walked forward and spoke.

"Yes Boris. It is your duty, as it was my duty, as it is the duty of every prince. I know you did not ask for this burden, but there is no point in complaining because it is the nature of the world."

"But why? Who made these rules? Why can't I just go and live as a wolf like I want to?"

Boris didn't notice how Shane and Eric glanced uncomfortably at each other.

"Because there are two sides to you Boris and you cannot deny either of them. I have worked hard to ensure that Lycanthia is a place where wolves can feel safe at expressing themselves again, but you should be at peace with both halves of your soul. It's…" Eric hung his head. "It's complicated and there are other people that could explain it far greater than I could. How I wish Pontus were here…" here. Shane reached across and clasped Eric's hand. Boris had vague memories of Pontus, the old teacher. He had always been fond of Boris, but the young man's memories were not as fierce as those of his parents.

"What your father is trying to say is that we want you to be happy and we want you to know that we understand what you're going through. We're not doing this to be mean or to try and control your life. We just want to make sure that you're prepared for everything that's going to happen in the future. Now, it used to be a tradition that a great banquet was thrown in your honor where the most eligible maidens were brought to meet you and their fathers could make offers for marriage. It's quite clear that's not something that you'd be interested in, so we're not going to put you through that," Shane said. Boris breathed a sigh of relief. "But you must at least consider the matter and start to be mindful of the future."

"The future...always the future. You've always told me to look to the future. When I was younger you told me that I was going to be special and learn to do all these amazing things. I still remember when you shifted in front of me father and told me that one day I would be just like you. And then you told me that I needed to learn to be a king and to look after my people. And now you tell me that I need to think about the person I'm going to marry. Sometimes I wonder what the point of living is, if so much has been decided for me!" Boris burst in anger.

Eric walked forward and put his hand on Boris' shoulder. "Believe me, nothing ever works out the way we plan, but it is always a good thing to be prepared. We have always tried to show you the good things that life has to offer. We have always tried to be honest with you and have never hid what is expected of you. I know it is not easy and I wish I could find a way to explain things so that you could understand. All we are asking is that you keep these things in mind."

Boris shrugged away his father's hand. "I just wish for once I was able to enjoy the present without having to worry about what I'm supposed to be doing or who I'm supposed to be. All the time you tell me to be mindful of the future and where I'm going and who I'm going to end up with, but I don't even know who I am!"

Shane and Eric fell silent. His parents were well-meaning, but there were times when he wished he had a brother or a sister to share the load. Being the son of a king was a lonely proposition. He had been tutored individually and while he had been given interactions with other children, he wasn't the same as them. They all knew that he was different and treated him as such. Some let him win because they thought they ought to as he was a royal, while others went in harder as they were envious of him and wanted to prove that just because he was a royal it didn't make him better than them.

"I'm sorry we haven't been able to give you a better life. We've both been trying to do what we can to ensure your happiness. We knew there would be difficulties. It might not seem like it to you, but we had to deal with our fair share when we were your age," Shane said.

"At one point we didn't think we'd actually be able to end up together. If it hadn't been for you, we might not have had the life we wanted," Eric said. Boris looked surly. He had heard this all before, but it didn't help him. They had gotten through their sorrow. They had ended up with the person they were meant to be with and they were happy. It was easier for them than it was for him.

"Let's just forget about this for the time being," Shane said. "Enjoy the gathering tonight and we'll figure something out. I was actually thinking that perhaps it would be good for you to get out of Lycanthia for a little while. Perhaps you could go and visit your mother. Sometimes it can take a trip away to make you realize everything that you have at home."

Boris' 'mother' was Triss Svensson, a native of Lycanthia that Eric and Shane trusted with their secret. Boris had met her a few times. She had an adventurous spirit and longed to see the world. She was different to every other woman that Eric had been introduced to, and she knew his secret; that he was gay. Once Shane discovered that he was pregnant, Eric and he had implored Triss for her help. Eric and Triss had gotten married in front of everyone, although the ceremony had been a mere illusion. The real marriage had been between Shane and Eric. Then, while Shane was growing Boris, Triss pretended that she was pregnant. Boris was presented as her child to keep the lie safe. Then, in time, Triss faded from view and went about her own business, traveling the world and operating the antique store that Shane had bequeathed to her, a store that had been opened by Boris' namesake.

She rarely returned to Lycanthia, but when she did, she always had an interesting story to tell and out of habit Boris called her Mom. He liked seeing her, but the thought of leaving Lycanthia left a bitter taste in his mouth.

"Why would I want to leave here? The rest of the world is backwards. I can't be a wolf out there. I don't want to have to hide who I am," Boris said. "I don't want any part of the human world. I'm not welcome there, so it's not welcome to me either," he said. Shane recoiled and looked hurt. He made some excuse and left the room. Boris felt a little guilty, but he hardened his expression, not wanting to show any weakness.

"You should be careful about what you say Boris," Eric said. "I know you are in love with being a wolf, but you are a human too. You should not neglect that. It hurts your father."

"I know. But I remember what it was like when you took me there as a child. You told me all these rules about what to hide from them and what not to say, and how I couldn't see you shift because the people out there didn't understand. It never made sense to me. Why would they be so afraid of us?"

"Because they don't understand us, and sadly humans have a propensity for reacting with fear to anything they don't understand. I would love for us to be able to go about our business without having to worry about what other people are going to do, but we simply don't have that luxury. I have to strike a balance between us being able to meet as a pack and keeping our existence a secret. I don't want anything to jeopardize our existence."

"You're the king. You can do anything you want. You should make it a law that people can't discriminate against wolves."

"And if I did that, we would garner far more attention than we can handle. Unfortunately the world is filled with greedy people who would like nothing more than to hunt us and put our furs up on the wall as trophies, or to study and dissect us, to try and find out what makes us work."

"What does make us work?" Boris asked.

"Magic," Eric replied. Boris knew he was going to say that, and he rolled his eyes. He was getting tired of hearing that answer.

"I just hate that the world has to be the way it is."

"I know you do. I did when I was your age, but you also have to accept that there are things you don't understand yet. You're still young and there is much for you to learn. I know it seems like the answers are straightforward. You want to cut through things in a straight line, but there are other considerations to make, and that is part of being a king, and being mature. You need to think of a world outside yourself and your own desires. I think you should go and visit Triss. She would be grateful of your visit and it would do you the world of good to see a new place and get a taste of the wider world. It might grant you a new perspective on things, and I know your father would appreciate it too. That store means a lot to him."

"Okay," Boris replied in a huff. Despite his somewhat bullish attitude he did hate making his parents sad. "I'll go and talk to him now. Oh, and Father, did you ever have strange dreams?" Boris asked.

"I think everyone has strange dreams from time to time."

"But what about ones that feel real?"

"No...I can't say that I have. Dreams are just dreams. They don't mean anything," Eric said. Boris nodded, but he couldn't agree. The sight of the shackled wolves still made him shudder and the fear gnawed at his heart. It felt as though there was something he was missing. So far, in all his training, nobody had ever mentioned dreams being a part of his werewolf nature. It made him wonder if there was something different about him, or something wrong. He made a point to ask Freya about it at the gathering. If anyone knew, she would.

But first he went to find Shane to apologize for his overreaction. Shane was standing on a balcony overlooking the gardens. The landscape was filled with beautiful flowers, and Boris' enhanced senses could even get a hint of the lingering scent. A few people walked around the gardens. The castle was always open to the people of Lycanthia and they took great joy in exploring the gardens. Lovers strolled along, lost in their own world, while kids played and ran in among the plants, infuriating the gardeners who were trying to keep everything tidy. Beyond the castle walls lay the sloping hills and deep valleys of Lycanthia. It was a beautiful place, and Boris couldn't understand why anyone would ever want to leave. The sky was sapphire blue and just a few wispy clouds covered the scene. The air was sweet. Birds soared through the sky, and a few insects buzzed around as they searched for something to feast on. Boris swept a hand in front of his face and swatted one away.

"I'm sorry for what I said father. I didn't mean to upset you."

"Oh no, it's alright," Shane said with a weak smile, turning to face Boris. His hands were placed on the balcony and he looked over the world like a caring observer. "I know that you don't have the same affinity as I do for the rest of the world."

"It's not that...I just don't like not being able to shift."

"I've always been sad that I haven't been able to experience that. It's been something that you and your father have shared and I...well, I know it's silly, but sometimes I'm sad that we haven't had anything like that."

"That's not true. We've had plenty. You've taught me a lot about life and you've always read me stories and you've always reminded me that honor and nobility come from your actions and beliefs, not just the fact that we live in a castle."

"That's true," Shane said, "but I know you prefer being a wolf to being a human."

Boris shifted his weight between his two feet and looked uncomfortable. He clasped his hands behind his back and picked at his nails. He chewed his bottom lip and cast his gaze to the shadowy part of the ground where a cat had flopped on its side, its tail idly swaying. It would have been easy to lie to his father and say that his human side was just as important to him as his wolf side, but his parents had always told him never to lie, especially not to them.

"It's not anything against you personally, it's just the way I feel," Boris said.

"I know, and I don't want to make you feel bad for it because it is who you are. I'm proud of you for embracing every aspect of yourself. There was someone a long time ago, a wolf who hated being a wolf. He wasn't happy and he hurt people because he wanted to free himself of his nature. I'm glad you are not like him. I just wish..." Shane sighed, "I wish that you could understand that life is a balance, and that there is still a lot of history in your human half as well. I never had much in the way of ancestry. I only learned about my parents when I was your age, and the only thing I really have in this world is that store. I know it's not much and it's certainly not as exciting as being able to shift into a wolf, but it's all I have to give you."

Boris was humbled when he listened to his father's words. He had heard the story of his grandparents multiple times, both from his parents and from Freya. It had been one of Freya's regrets; she had been so paranoid she thought Shane's parents were a threat when in fact they had just wanted to explore the rumors and find out the truth about Lycanthia. But Freya had captured them and put them in chains. Shane's father had been killed in an attempt to escape, and his mother had lost her mind. When she had given birth to Shane, Freya intended to keep the child imprisoned too, but some wolves did not agree with that. One of them, Boris, had fled Lycanthia with Shane and raised him as his own son. That was the man the prince was named after.

Sometimes Boris found it difficult to believe Freya could be so cruel and callous, but there were moments when she spoke to him sharply or glared at someone who displeased her, and her expression changed into something spiteful. Then, he truly was afraid of her and could believe that she had done these terrible things, although she had done them in the name of defending her people.

"It does mean a lot to me father, and I do want to visit the store again. I know sometimes I can seem ungrateful and I'm sorry for that. It's just a confusing time. It appears everyone has an idea of what they want me to be, and I don't have an answer for that myself. That's why I like being a wolf. It's much simpler. It comes easy to me and I'm never filled with doubt and I never have to worry that I'm doing the wrong thing or disappointing people."

Shane turned around fully and placed both hands on Boris' shoulders. He had to tilt his head back for Boris' physique was so impressive that he had already overtaken his father in height, although he was still a few inches away from Eric's.

"You never have to worry that you're disappointing us. You are everything that we could have hoped for. We love you with all our hearts and we're so, so proud of the man you're growing into," Shane said. Boris smiled and wished that he could feel the same way. There was something inside him that kept gnawing at him and nagging him, telling him that he wasn't as good as he should have been. What Shane said was sweet, but Boris knew that he made their lives difficult. He could have made life easier for them and declared that he was happy to be married as soon as possible, he could have accepted his duties and responsibilities without complaint too, but it didn't feel real to him. It felt as though he was putting on a performance.

Would the confusion ever end?

***

Thankfully Boris had the gathering to look forward to. Spending time with the other wolves always served to help take his mind off the things that troubled him. Tonight was no exception. As soon as night fell and the moon rose, as soon as Lycanthia was shrouded in darkness and the quiet solitude of the night fell like a blanket over everyone, the wolves started to make their way to the forest in droves. It was a ritual that took place every couple of weeks or so and had begun again when Boris had been presented to them as a baby. While he didn't remember that first one, the memories as a child had always been happy ones. The atmosphere was that of a festival as the wolves were free to shed their human forms and indulge their primal desires. They ran as one, streaming through the forest, and it became alive with the sounds of their howls. It made Boris' heart thrum when he was around them. He had never felt as alive as he did when he was with the wolves, and he was eager to see them again.

He ran along with Eric, panting with glee as he tried to outpace his father. For a moment he thought he might be able to do so, until Eric showed a startling burst of speed to overtake him and reach the pack before he did. Boris playfully growled, but then took up his position at the head of the pack alongside his father, the alpha. They led the pack through the forest. The bracken crackled under the thunder of their paws. The air was alive with howls and all the other animals scurried away out of fear. Whenever the pack ran, they owned the forest, and all other life disappeared.

While there were regular humans who lived in Lycanthia, none dared to enter the woods when the howls of the wolves were heard. It was as though the wolves had the whole world to themselves, and it was exactly the kind of life that Boris wanted. He didn't have to worry about keeping secrets or feeling constrained by his own body. He could be free to shift as often as he wanted, or as often as he could.

They sprinted for a long time all around the forest, moving in a wide circle, until they ended up in among trees. There was a copse where ancient stones stood, stones that had spiritual significance to the wolves. There, some elders waited for them, along with Freya. He felt sorry for his grandmother. Although he had only enjoyed the freedom of being a wolf for a short time, he couldn't imagine having the ability to shift stripped away from him. Some of the other wolves walked up to her and licked her hand, paying her respects. Boris waited a few moments and then approached her himself, shifting back into a human so that he could talk with her.

"Are you in good spirits tonight Boris?" Freya asked.

"I am actually, are you?"

"It always fills me with pleasure to see the pack together like this. There was a time when I forgot just how many of us there were," she said.

"It's something that brings me great joy too. There is something I want to talk to you about thought. It's about what the wolves are capable of. You keep telling me that there is much I need to learn, but is there anything specific you think I should know? Something more than what I know already? Perhaps something even...magical? Something to do with dreams?"

"Dreams?" Freya had a thoughtful look on her face. "A long time ago there were seers, but there has not been one for generations. Why do you ask?"

"I was thinking about some of the stories father used to tell me and there were always magical abilities involved with creatures like us. I just wondered if there was anything I should know about, or anything that might need training," he said. "But these seers seem interesting. Are there any that exist now? What happened to them?"

Freya studied him and he wondered if he was being too zealous in his desire to press her for information. "Those stories are just that, stories. There is no reason to think that they mean anything else. All I meant when I said there is more for you to learn, it's about the world as a whole and your place in it. I know you do not like hearing that you are still a child, but learning is a constant process. I still had a lot to learn even when you were born. Your fathers taught me a great deal. Anyway, the seers…well…there certainly aren't any around now, or if they are, they're keeping themselves quiet. I haven't known any personally. They were said to exist a long time ago, but whether they actually did or not, I can't say for certain. I wouldn't trust them anyway. Dreams are always vague and tricky things. Better to go on cold hard facts, there's no chance of misinterpreting them" she said with a cackling laugh and a tap of her cane on the ground. There were other people vying for her attention, so Boris took his leave and walked away, somewhat disappointed.

Maybe he was just reaching to be special, maybe these dreams meant nothing, but how was he supposed to know if nobody could help him? He walked away to sit on a log and watched the night unfold. The wolves were all in good spirits. He was about to shift back into his lycan form to push away all the doubts that plagued him, when another wolf padded up to him and shifted before his eyes. It was his good friend Peter, who smiled when he regained his human form.

"How are you doing tonight?" Peter asked. He was of a similar age to Boris. They had known each other a long time though, as both had been brought to the gathering as children, and both had expressed their dismay and frustration at not being able to partake in the festivities until they were eighteen. He was shorter than Boris and had pale skin with fair hair. Freckles dusted his nose and cheeks.

"I'm doing just fine. I tell you what, these things take on a different atmosphere when you can actually shift," Boris said.

"I was thinking the same thing. When I'm here I'm not sure that I ever want to go back to my normal life again," Peter replied.

"And how is the fishing trade treating you?"

Peter shrugged. "It's okay, I guess. It's a bit like hunting, although I'm not a big fan of the water. But it's nice to be out on the sea and look at the world around us. You'll have to come out one day and see what happens for yourself. It's exciting when we get a big haul."

"I think I'll pass on that offer, thanks all the same," Boris said with a warm smile. "I just like being here, in this place. I'd love to live like this all the time. Imagine just being wolves whenever we like and not having to worry about anything else we have to do."

"It's a nice dream, but not very practical. We have bills to pay and homes to look after, and why are you saying that, you're going to be a King!"

Boris arched his eyebrows. "It's not as exciting as you think Peter. There are times when I wish I weren't a prince at all, although don't tell anyone I said that."

"I won't. You know you can trust me with anything," Peter said.

Boris smiled.

"You're a good friend Peter."

"My parents were talking today...they said that they're surprised there hasn't been a feast in your honor. They said that its tradition that all the maidens of the country are brought before you in the hope that you'll choose one of them to marry, just like what happened with your father and Triss."

"Yes, well, I don't think that's going to happen this year. There are some things that need to change with the times," Boris said. His lips were tight. The two men sat closely together, so close that their legs were touching and Boris could feel the heat that emanated from the other young man.

"But you'll need a wife...wont' you?"

"I suppose, in time, if I'm to have an heir," Boris sighed. He dipped his head and shook it. He leaned down and picked up a small twig from the ground and broke it in two. It made a sharp crack. "But the truth is I don't want anything to do with all that. It's all a big distraction that just takes our attention away from the important things. I wish that it didn't have to be a part of my life. I'd much rather just be alone and have friendships like you and I have. That seems much better than some silly romance. What good does it do anyone?" Boris was so caught up in his own feelings and his own emotions that he didn't notice Peter shifting uncomfortably on the log, or the uneasy expression that came upon his face.

"I don't know...I think it's nice to share your life with someone and to have someone you can share your innermost feelings with. Sometimes it can get lonely being by yourself and only having your own thoughts rolling around in your mind."

"But in that case, we have things like this now!" Boris scoffed. "No, I think romance is one of the biggest wastes of time there ever is in the world. It's all a big lie that people tell each other they need when not everyone needs it. I'm sure for some people it's necessary, but not for me. I'll be fine by myself, and I'm half-tempted to stay by myself just to prove everyone wrong."

"I don't know if I could live like that," Peter said in a small voice, "but I suppose you have to do what you think is best." He shifted himself away from Boris and turned his face away. Boris creased his brow in confusion and couldn't understand why Peter had changed in mood so dramatically. Before either of them had a chance to speak, another wolf came up to them. This one was black and lean. If it weren't for the golden shine of the wolf's eyes, he would have blended into the night perfectly.

When he shifted, he turned into a lean, pale man with striking features and long fingers. His body was thin like willow, and when he spoke it was in a soft, velvet voice that meant Boris had to lean in to hear properly. He vaguely recognized the man from previous gatherings, although he couldn't remember being formally introduced to him.

"Ah, Peter, there you are. And Prince Boris, it's an honor to see you. I'm Byron." He held out his hand. It was surprisingly cold. Byron's thin lips stretched into a smile, although it looked unnatural on his face, as though he was just practicing an imitation of a smile. "I'm sorry for interrupting, but I wanted to introduce myself to you properly. I have only been to a few of these gatherings since I have returned home to Lycanthia and thought it best to pay my respects to the Crown Prince," he swept his arm across his waist and bowed.

"You're welcome, although you don't need to bother with all the proper etiquette. We're not in the castle," Boris said. "How do you two know each other?"

"Byron is my uncle," Peter said. "He knows about a lot of things. He's traveled all around the world."

"Really?" Byron gasped.

"I wouldn't say all around, but yes I've seen a few more places. Peter, I believe your mother wanted to speak to you," Byron gestured behind him. Peter looked sullen as he hopped off the log and walked away. Byron remained standing, looming over Boris, and continued speaking. "My sister was adamant that I should return as things had changed here. I wasn't sure if I should come back, but I'm glad I did. Things have certainly changed for the better. It's nice to see all these wolves in the same place," he said.

"It is. My father is responsible," Boris said, puffing out his chest as he boasted.

Byron's eyes twinkled. "He is a wise, strong ruler indeed. It runs in the family," Byron twisted his head back and glanced toward Freya. Boris didn't catch the hint of bitterness that laced his words. "I did just pay my respects to Freya as well, although I haven't had the honor of seeing your father yet. But there is time for that. Peter speaks very highly of you whenever he has the chance. I think it's wonderful that you have each other as a companion to go through this process. It can be a strange and confusing time when everything is new."

"Yes, it can be," Boris said, and he started to become a little wary of the way Byron was talking. But Byron didn't seem deterred.

"I hope you'll forgive me, but I couldn't help overhearing your conversation with Freya earlier. I believe you were asking about seers and the meaning of dreams?" Byron said.

"I was," Boris said, and he clenched his teeth for he was not fond of other people listening in on his private conversations, especially not when it dealt with something as sensitive as his dreams. But then Byron said something that made Boris stiffen and take note.

"As much as Freya is wise, I do believe that her insistence on staying in Lycanthia has hurt her perception of things. There are seers in the world. I have known a few of them."

"Really?" Boris said in a rush of breath.

"Oh yes. Us wolves are capable of a great many things, but sadly some of the knowledge has been lost over time," he hung his head in a grave manner, as though it was a great tragedy. "But in other parts of the world such knowledge still exists. I tried to learn as much as I could about these matters-"

"Do you think you could teach me?" Boris asked quickly, desperately. Byron arched an eyebrow and paced before Boris, considering the matter.

"That is quite a prospect. I didn't intend to teach anyone when I returned here. Frankly I wasn't sure that anyone would want to know what I had learned."

"I need a teacher. My grandmother has been teaching me most of what I need to learn, but if you know things she doesn't, it can only be a good thing. There are so many things I've been wondering about, so many questions I want the answers to! Please, you must agree. If I must, I shall make it a royal order!"

"Well, in that case, who am I to refuse the wishes of the Crown Prince? I would be honored to teach you," Byron bowed again, and Boris looked satisfied. This was just what he needed, a teacher who knew things that nobody else did. He might be the key that Boris needed to unlock the mysteries of his people, and the mystery of his own mind.

"Come by the castle tomorrow and we shall begin," Boris declared. Byron nodded and then walked away. Boris felt a little better. He searched for Peter, but the other wolf had disappeared. The night was young and Boris wanted to seize as much of it as he could. He gave into the wolf and led a few other wolves on a race through the forest. Branches whipped his skin as he careened past trees and now, he truly was looking to the future, because he hoped he would gain a better understanding of himself.

Chapter Four

Byron had instructed Tristan to busy himself studying while he went to the gathering. Tristan sat in his small room gazing out of the window at the twinkling stars and the bright moon. The silver light poured down upon the world as though someone had tipped over a mug that had been filled with shining liquid steel and it had all flowed over the landscape. Tristan sighed a little as it made him nostalgic for the broad moors of the English countryside. That had been his home for as long as he could remember and while it was comforting for Byron to be back in Lycanthia, it wasn't the same for Tristan.

It also galled him that he couldn't go to the gathering with Byron. No humans were allowed as it was a wolf-only affair. Not even the King's closest friend was allowed. Tristan had listened intently as Emilia had enlightened Byron on the structure of the royal court. King Magnus had died some years ago and Eric had taken the throne, and by all accounts he was a wise and noble king. Queen Freya, who had taken care of Lycanthia ever since the death of her father, had stepped back and allowed her son to rule. She still wielded much influence within the court, and with the wolves. The actual Queen, Triss, was absent from the court. Apparently, according to Emilia, the woman had always been a free spirit and never liked being tied down to anything. It had been quite the surprise when it was announced that she would marry Prince Eric, as nobody had thought her suited for the role of a Queen, nobody except Eric at least. It didn't seem to be a discordant separation though as Triss came to visit on occasion, but it was an odd situation. The King spent most of his time with Shane, and there were suspicions that the two of them were involved in a romance. It was only idle gossip though, and as far as Emilia was concerned the romantic relationship of the royals wasn't any concern of hers.

Tristan did find it fascinating though. His life had been a solitary one and thus he had always been intrigued by the interpersonal relationships of people. It was a strange concept to him. He had rarely been around people his own age, and most of the work he had done with Byron had only involved the two of them. To be in this thriving town with life all around them was daunting and exhilarating in equal measure. He was determined to adjust though and show Byron that he was capable of anything. After all he was a wolf in spirit if not in blood, and wolves could cope with anything.

As he gazed out of the window, he thought about them all running together in a pack. There was a deep longing in his heart as he envied them. His parents had been taken from him at a young age. Byron was the only family he had, but to be a part of something much bigger was incredible, and Tristan wished he could experience something like that.

But he couldn't.

He was a wolf, so he wasn't able to enjoy that privilege.

He thought about what Byron had said concerning the royal family. The current prince, Boris, was perhaps the more fortunate man in the world. Not only did he have the benefit of living in the castle as part of the royal family, but he also had lycan blood running through his veins. He had the best of both worlds, and Tristan felt his heart burn with enmity for the man.

To busy himself, Tristan pulled out some books about old artifacts and pored over them, reading by candlelight. He made his way through the pages carefully, for they were old and fragile. One tight tug would have been enough to rip them from the spine. The parchment was faded and stained. The ink was difficult to read, but Tristan had patience and he was used to examining books like these. He carefully passed through lots of entries, some of which did look interesting, but he was after something specific.

His eyes lit up when he found it.

The page was dwarfed by an illustration of the chalice. It had a long stem and jewels were embedded around the main body. There were intricate carvings on it, although of course the color of the illustration had faded over time, leaving it looking grey and dull. Around the illustration was writing about the chalice. Said to have been enchanted by a sorcerer called Sinterbaum, the chalice had the ability to turn a mortal into a wolf, or vice versa. It seemed so easy, although of course magic was never easy. But to think that all he had to do was sip from a chalice and his greatest dreams could come true...it was almost unbelievable.

Because of the nature of the chalice there was some confusion as to whether Sinterbaum had been in favor of the wolves or an enemy. Tristan looked through a number of other books to see if he could glean any other information about the man, but there were barely any other references to him, and the ones that were present in the texts he examined were vague and uninformative. Tristan sat back in his chair and digested all he had read. It was a marvel to think of the world that had been lost to time, a world when wolves were in their prime and could roam freely, until they had to flee to Lycanthia because they had been hunted.

Tristan found himself growing angry at the narrow mindedness displayed by his ancestors. If they had been more trusting of the wolves everyone might have been able to have these abilities. As far as Tristan saw it the werewolves were a gift, blending humanity with nature and it was something that shouldn't be ignored. He was certain that Sinterbaum couldn't have been the only person to desire a change in the balance of nature, and if so, someone else must have made something to turn people into wolves.

He had to get in that castle and see the relics on display.

***

"I have wonderful news!" Byron said as returned from the gathering. Tristan had lost track of time and stayed up long past he was tired. His stamina was greater than most humans thanks to the potions that Byron made for him, but he still required rest. He looked up from his books with a vague expression on his face. Usually, Byron would have scolded him, but on this occasion, Byron seemed too excited for that to happen.

"I take it the gathering went well?" Tristan asked.

"Oh yes. It went better as I expected. As I suspected, much has been lost since the wolves were isolated. So much knowledge has been forgotten. It is a great shame, but it does mean that we have returned at the right time to make a difference. I even managed to see Freya, although she did not remember. It just goes to show how little she pays attention to the wolves who mean nothing to her. I was never a part of the noble circle, so why should she bother with me? But that is all going to change now. I spoke with the prince himself and he seems rather eager to learn what I can teach him. I'm going to become his tutor, and you are going to help. I want you there by my side for all the lessons. I want to befriend the prince, because there are things he will tell his friend that he would never tell his teacher, and possibly not even his father. We shall move into the castle as well I expect so we won't have to deal with these dull dwellings," he cast a dismissive hand around the room.

"I shall do whatever you ask," Tristan said.

"You are such an obedient young man. I could not ask for a better ward. Now then, I must prepare, yes, I must think of what to teach him. It should not be anything too controversial to begin with. I would hate to garner too much attention from his father or grandmother," Byron muttered to himself. He rubbed his fingers together before turning to the shelves of books and pulling a few down from the shelves. Tristan had seen this behavior often. Byron was lost in his own mind and there was no real need for Tristan to stick around, so he dragged himself to bed and fell asleep looking toward the stars, in the vague direction of where he suspected England lay. This new task ensured that their stay in Lycanthia would not be a short one, and it meant that Tristan would have to spend even longer away from home.

He sighed as he sank into the pillow and thought of the future, a brighter future where he might get everything he ever wanted, where he might become a wolf.

***

Byron awoke him bright and early. Tristan jumped out of bed and splashed some water on his face. Byron had arranged a stack of books that he thought would make a good curriculum. Tristan looked at them with wide eyes, worrying that he was going to have to be the one who carried them to the castle. When he voiced this concern, Byron laughed so hard he put his hands across his belly, and informed Tristan that there would be people from the castle who could do all the menial tasks for them. He put his hand around Tristan's shoulders and told the boy that their lives would never be the same again.

Tristan believed him, just as he believed Byron in all matters.

They were soon on their way to the castle.

"Don't worry about feeling daunted. It's quite natural. The place is huge and there are going to be a lot of people there. Just stick close to me and don't worry about anything. People aren't going to be too bothered by you as long as you don't disturb them. I'd suggest taking everything in. This is a good learning opportunity, so don't let it slip past you," Byron instructed.

Tristan nodded and tried to quell the rising nerves in the pit of his stomach. The castle loomed above them, made of grey stone and gleaming windows. Tristan immediately bristled with the sight of so many people around him. The bustling crowd nudged into him and he exclaimed in surprise, but Byron didn't suffer from the same thing. Tristan had to put in serious effort to keep up with his mentor, until they eventually found themselves in the throne room. The king was sitting on the throne, a magnificent man who was so handsome that Tristan's breath caught in his throat. Beside the king was another man, Shane, and then sitting to the side was Boris, the prince. As Tristan's gaze fell upon the prince his body was filled with warmth and an uncomfortable feeling settled in the pit of his stomach. The prince was the spitting image of his father; more handsome than anyone Tristan had seen before, and the fact that the prince was a wolf only added to his allure.

Tristan's blood sang with arousal and he struggled to not make it obvious that he was enthralled with the prince. Upon seeing Byron enter the room, the prince leaped up and looked enthused.

"This is Byron, the man I was telling you about. He volunteered to be my tutor," Boris said. He walked up to Byron and shook his hand eagerly. He quickly glanced at Tristan, but his gaze did not linger on Byron's ward.

"Your majesty, it is an honor to be in your presence and yes," Byron said as he bowed. Tristan mimicked the movement. "I did volunteer, although I hope it was not unbecoming of me. I have always been a scholar on matters of the past and I believe that I could teach your prince a great deal about the history of Lycanthia."

"Indeed," Eric leaned forward and raised his hand to rest against his chin. His brow furrowed underneath the golden band that was his crown, and a thoughtful expression came across his face. "He needs a new tutor. I do like that Boris has a desire to increase his knowledge, but it is a privileged position. I hope you do not take offence to my saying so, but you are a stranger to me, and I am not in the habit of appointing strangers to my court."

"Of course, your grace, but although I am a stranger to you, I am not a stranger to the kingdom of Lycanthia. The blood of our ancestors flows through my veins and I am proud of my heritage. I was here when your grandfather met his unfortunate end, and I mourned along with everyone else. After that tragedy, Lycanthia's purity was tainted and I found myself longing for something else, so I set my sights on the rest of the world. I knew there was still much for me to learn and experience. I thought that by doing so I would be able to serve my country upon my return. We are a small country and few of us ever leave to explore the wider world. I wanted to change that. I have many tomes of knowledge and a wide understanding of a great many different concepts that should help enlighten the young prince's mind."

"Please father," Boris interjected, "You know I've always longed to learn from someone who has traveled the world. It's so rare for one us to have seen so much. I could learn a lot from Byron, I just know it. At least give him a chance."

Eric listened to his son's words, but his inscrutable gaze fell upon Byron and Tristan once again.

"And who is this?" Eric asked, opening his palm to gesture at Tristan. Heat rose to Tristan's cheeks as he stepped forward and bowed.

"This is my trusted ward Tristan. He has been with me all his life, and I kept him on after a terrible tragedy took his parents from the world. I have taught him everything I know, and he helps me in my endeavors. You will not find a more loyal or honorable man in all the world," Byron said. Tristan smiled at the boast, although he didn't feel deserving of the words. The story seemed to have an effect on Shane. The man sitting next to Eric immediately leaned over and whispered something in the King's ear. Tristan's gaze once again drifted over to the prince, and he was amazed that anyone could be in the same room with that magnificent man and not be focused on him. The prince had a bright glow about him, almost as though he was a god. His thick hair glinted red in the sun, and he stood in a powerful stance, as though he knew that the world would bend to his will if he tried. He looked earnestly at the king, and his eyes gleamed with hope.

"Very well," the King said. "Please proceed, although I shall want regular updates to make sure that this is of benefit to the prince. I will also require an overview of what you plan to teach my son. I will arrange quarters for you and your ward, and a suitable room that will be used for tutoring, and to store all these tomes you're bringing with you. It is an opportune time actually. You can set up in the castle while Boris takes a trip to see his mother in America."

Tristan was probably the only person in the room to see Byron blanch. His mentor was a man who liked being in control of his schedule and he never did well when other people dictated a routine to him. It was evident to Tristan in the way that Byron held himself rigidly, and how his lips twitched ever so slightly.

"Of course, your Grace, although could I ask you for Tristan to accompany the Prince? It would do him the world of good to experience a trip like this, and it would give the prince some company."

Tristan looked across at the prince, expecting him to smile, but the prince scowled. The King looked uneasy for a moment, when Byron spoke again. "I should mention that Tristan knows all of my secrets your Highness. I keep nothing from him, and he is very discreet. He knows the rules by which all those who live in Lycanthia abide." This seemed to satisfy the King and he nodded, agreeing to the proposal. Eric rolled his eyes, but Tristan was secretly delighted. As soon as this was agreed Byron bowed again and left the throne room with Tristan in tow.

***

"That went even better than expected! Perhaps the King is not such a fool as his mother. He knows to surround his son with the best people. Tristan, I shall stay here and prepare things for your return. While you are away, I want you to endear yourself to the prince. Make yourself invaluable to him. If we are to learn more about the inner workings of the castle his information will be vital. We need to ensure we are indispensable to the prince, as I fear that once we get to the advanced lessons, his father and grandmother may have something to say about the subject matter…"

"What do you mean by that?" Tristan asked.

"Oh, that's nothing for you to worry about that. Just enjoy your trip and when I come back, I want the two of you to be the firmest of friends."

Tristan nodded although it was something certainly easier said than done. He couldn't remember the last time he had made a real friend. Their trips to other countries were always brief and they rarely worked with other people. This was entirely new territory for Tristan to explore, and he wasn't sure how to succeed. But he knew he was blessed at being able to spend some time with the prince, and he wanted it to count for something.

Chapter Five

Boris and Tristan met at the airport and got onto the private jet. Boris had been looking forward to a solo trip to America where he could be by himself and think about matters, but at the last instant his new tutor had insisted on the ward joining him. Perhaps Byron wasn't going to be as useful as Boris first imagined. Tristan was quiet and pale. He was tall and lean, and the clothes he wore seemed ill-fitting and they were mismatched. Boris could tell that he had never had a tailor. Tristan offered him an awkward smile as they walked onto the plane, which Boris returned out of politeness. He wasn't entirely sure what to say to Tristan and when he took his seat on the plane, he intended to spend the trip in silence.

However, the tension on the plane soon became awkward. Boris noticed that Tristan was always looking at him, and whenever Boris went to meet his gaze, Tristan's eyes darted away. It became something of a game for Boris and he found it amusing. But the longer they remained silent the more Boris grew frustrated with himself. He wasn't prepared to spend the rest of the flight in silence, so he took it upon himself to initiate something that would keep the both of them occupied. It was a thin ploy from his parents to try and get him used to spending time with other people, but Boris would indulge them on this instance. He assumed their minds had been made up as soon as Byron had revealed that Tristan knew all about the secrets of Lycanthia so there wasn't any worry about Boris letting the truth slip out. Furthermore, Tristan was a human, and Shane probably thought that it would do Boris some good to spend time with a pureblood mortal.

"So, what exactly does a ward do?" Boris asked.

Tristan licked his lips nervously, as though he hadn't expected Boris to ask him a question.

"Just about anything that Byron asks me to do. I help him research and explore the world. I take notes for him and discuss the relevant issues that we explore. I've been all over the world with him. I've helped him as we explored ancient ruins and dug for artifacts. I've translated ancient tomes, and I've taken part in experiments and spells."

Boris was impressed. Perhaps Tristan was not going to be such boring company as he feared.

"Where in the world have you been? What kind of things have you seen? I've barely been anywhere but Lycanthia."

"But you're a prince. You could go anywhere you wanted."

"That is true, to a certain extent, but I haven't wanted to go anywhere else. Lycanthia is my home and it has everything I've ever wanted. But there is a part of me that has always been curious. I'm sure that my mother will enjoy hearing your stories as well. She always wanted to go to different countries."

"I'm not sure that I have many exciting stories…we've just been to different places and found a few different relics. Mostly we just study them and try to figure out where they came from and what their link to history is. We look through books we have and identify them, catalogue them, and then we know where they came from. But what you said interests me. I was surprised when I found out that your mother lives in another country. How does that work? Why does she leave?"

"It's a long story," Boris said, looking away. "She just had other plans for her life and never really wanted to bother with all the official things that came with being Queen. She wasn't suited for it, so she and my father decided that it was best for her to be happy."

"But don't you miss her?"

"Of course, but I see her now and then and what's more important is that she's happy. Besides my father loves me enough to make up for it," Boris said. His heart ached for the fact that he couldn't tell Tristan the truth. He wanted to declare that he loved his other father with all his heart, and that he wanted for nothing as both his parents had doted on him and adored him all his life. But he couldn't. That was a part of the pact, and he had to do everything he could to stop Tristan from exploring down this pathway. But it was Tristan who spoke next.

"I was surprised that your father let me accompany you," Tristan said. "Especially if you're going on a rare visit to your mother. I hope I'm not intruding."

"You're not, and I'm not surprised. As soon as Byron told them your story, I knew it was certain. You see my father's…dear friend Shane suffered a similar fate to yours. His parents died when he was very young and he grew up under the care of someone else, someone who had exiled himself from Lycanthia. I think he sees something of himself in you," Boris had to remember to be very careful with what he said. The secret of his lycan nature did not have to be shielded, but the secret about his parentage did.

"Does he know about you all?" Tristan asked.

"Whatever do you mean?" Boris asked, leaning back in his chair, arching his eyebrow playfully. He folded his arms across his chest and almost dared Tristan to say the words, wondering if he would. Tristan squirmed and Boris enjoyed this, but not in a mean, cruel way. It was just fun to be able to play with someone's expectations.

"You know what I mean."

"I have no idea. I don't know what Byron has told you," Boris said in a tone that showed he knew exactly what he was doing. Tristan furrowed his brow and scowled. He leaned forward and shadows come under his eyes. At that point Boris was shocked as there was something familiar about Tristan, something that he couldn't place, but it was a profound feeling and it thrummed right through the core of his body. Thankfully, he was used to playing his cards close to his chest and managed to keep his emotions hidden.

"Fine, does he know that you're all werewolves?" Tristan asked in a defeated tone. Boris smiled to himself. It was Shane, of course, who had played an important role in helping bring the wolves back into the light again.

"Yes, he does. My father trusts him more than anyone else in the world. As do I, actually. He's like family," Boris said, figuring that was the closest he could get to the truth without actually admitting it. "What happened to your parents?" Boris asked, trying to ease the conversation away from tentative subjects.

Tristan shifted in his seat and continued to lean forward. He rested his elbows on his knees and clasped his hands together. A sorrowful expression came upon his face and when he spoke his words were heavy with emotion. He looked as though he had aged about ten years and Boris became aware of the burden that he carried on his shoulders.

"It happened when I was younger. I wasn't even ten. They had worked with Byron for a long time. One night he was conducting an experiment and had left it to simmer. My parents went in to investigate and they must have tampered with some ingredient or the experiment chose that moment to misfire. It killed them. I woke up to Byron telling me the terrible news. I didn't know what to do. I didn't believe it at first, not until he showed me their graves. He had already taken the liberty to bury them."

"It's sad that you didn't even get to see them one last time."

"He said that the damage to their bodies was too great for me to see. He said it wasn't how they would want me to remember them. We stood there for a long time. I said goodbye. I wasn't sure what to say really. Byron told me that I would never have to worry about a thing. He said that he would always take care of me, and he has."

"I'm sorry," Boris said, his voice earnest and sincere. He leaned forward to mirror Tristan's posture and reached over, placing a hand on Tristan's shoulder. It was a simple gesture, and one that Boris wasn't even sure would make a difference, but he thought it was the least he could do as he felt a little guilty. There he was, feeling annoyed that he couldn't tell the truth about his parents without being grateful that he had both parents, and even a third in Triss. He was blessed, while Tristan had none. Boris knew well how much a lack of parents could affect someone. Shane had told him about how hard life had been, especially when he found out what had happened to his parents. That same pain was mirrored in Tristan. Shane had had Eric to help him through the pain, perhaps Boris could do something similar for Tristan. He had been irked at his parents' blatant attempts to get him to interact with other people, but perhaps having a friend wouldn't be such a bad thing.

"Is there anything you'd like to talk about? I know it can be hard…" Boris offered weakly. He hadn't taken the time to be a friend to many people and wasn't quite sure how to act. He tried to remember how his parents spoke to him whenever he was troubled.

Tristan sat back and inhaled deeply. "There is something actually…Byron mentioned that there are a lot of relics in the castle. I was wondering about one in particular…" Tristan said, trailing off.

"Yes?" Boris asked, a little puzzled because he had meant something emotional, but given that Tristan had found a great many artifacts it seemed natural that he would enquire about them.

"There's one that Byron mentioned, one that he thought was lost a long time ago. It was a chalice, a chalice of…it was a strange name, Sinterbaum I believe," Tristan said.

"Oh yeah, that's in the castle," Boris said, "But I don't think it's a relic. It's just a chalice. It's there for display more than anything. I don't think there's anything very special about it. Why do you ask about that in particular?"

Tristan licked his lips and smiled. "No reason really, it's just that I have a tendency to be intrigued by lost treasure. It's good to know that it was found," he said.

"I agree, now tell me about some of the things you've found. I am very interested in learning about our history. There must be a lot of things that I've never even heard of." Boris leaned forward eagerly and his eyes gleamed with curiosity as the plane rumbled over the Atlantic Ocean. The sky was a black sheet underneath them, and the lights on the plane were dim to mimic the evening.

Chapter Six

Tristan couldn't believe his luck. The Chalice of Sinterbaum wasn't lost at all. It was in the castle! At first, he was surprised that Boris treated the chalice with such a casual tone. It was one of the most powerful relics ever made, and he had no idea! Tristan had almost told Boris the truth, until he realized that he must have been kept in the dark for a reason. There was no way Freya, or the King, didn't know what the chalice could do, which meant they had willfully kept the truth from Boris. Byron would find that interesting, Tristan thought.

It was difficult to conduct this spy mission as it seemed unethical, but Tristan decided there was no harm. After all, Byron was just trying to ensure that the two of them had employment in the castle for the foreseeable future, and to spread their knowledge and wisdom. They were noble goals. Tristan did feel a natural affinity for the prince and being in such close proximity overwhelmed his senses. The air was alive with his musky, masculine scent, and when Boris had placed his hand on Tristan's shoulder, Tristan had tingled all over in a way that he never had before. It was as though his body had just come alive like a dormant volcano. Strange sensations swirled in the pit of his stomach and flowed through his limbs.

Boris was kind and attentive. He was everything a man should be, and in his body ran the blood of the wolf. Tristan felt it a privilege to be in his presence and as Boris leaned back in his chair and went to sleep, Tristan couldn't help but stare at him. The hum of the plane was quiet and lulling. Tristan gazed at the angles of Boris' face and how his lips were slightly parted. His chest rose and fell in rhythmic breathing. The shirt he wore was open at the collar and allowed

Tristan a glimpse at the chest underneath, and the thick bed of hair. It was a display of his masculinity and his bestial nature. Tristan could only imagine what Boris was like as a wolf. He must have been majestic. The image of him running through the world made something inside Tristan twitch. It was deep and dark, and the elated feeling rose through his body and seemed to reach out to the tips of his fingers. He started to tremble and pulled himself away, moving to the bathroom for some privacy.

The burning need was too powerful, too irresistible. His hands were trembling and he gasped as he reached down and took hold of his hard arousal. His eyes clamped shut as he thought about Boris and a smile played upon his lips. His cheeks became flushed as blood sang through his body. Groaning, he imagined a different path they could have taken earlier. When Boris placed his consoling arm upon Tristan's shoulder, Tristan imagined flinging himself at Boris, surprising him with a firm kiss. Boris would resist at first, of course, because it was wholly new and unexpected, but as their lips met in a sweet embrace, he would come to know it as bliss. Their breaths would mingle. Tristan's body tensed as he imagined the passion of the embrace. His hand moved furiously as the burning passion crashed through his body. The air around him felt as though it was on fire and he refused to open his eyes even though he could feel his eyelids flutter, for he did not want to tear himself away from this fantasy. In his mind it was a reality, so much so that he could almost feel Boris' warm flesh. Oh yes, if he could win the heart of the wolf, that would be something wonderful.

Tristan let out a low growl as all the sensations mixed into a powerful cocktail. His chest heaved and his breath tightened as he felt the ripples of pleasure become more frequent and more powerful. A light burst before his eyes and in one moment of pure radiant brilliance he knew paradise. His entire body thrummed with pleasure and he had to slam his hand against a wall to steady himself. His muscles pulsed with the energy it had taken to bring him to orgasm, and his head hung as he gulped in deep breaths to try and regain his composure.

But as he breathed, and as the intense feelings slipped away, reality came back into focus. Tristan knew that it had only been a fantasy. Boris was a wolf prince, and Tristan was a ward. What was the point in dreaming of the impossible? The dreamy haze of the orgasm was in stark contrast to the grim reality of the situation. The walls were narrow and the plane was suffocating. The rhythmic rumble of the engine was a constant drone. This is what his life would always be like unless he got the chalice.

His reflections were broken up by a loud shout coming from the plane. He rushed out of the bathroom and saw Boris jerking in his chair. Tristan rushed up to him. Boris was screaming loudly. His face was twisted in fear. His hands and legs writhed as though he was trying to shield himself from some invisible force. At first Tristan assumed Boris was awake, but his eyes were still closed. Tristan took hold of Boris' shoulders and shook him awake.

Boris' eyes were white with fear and it took him a few moments to realize what was happening. After regaining his equilibrium, he used Tristan's strength to sit up. He reached over and grabbed some water to drink, and then rubbed his face. His expression was still stricken with horror and he had to take a few deep breaths to compose himself. He looked around frantically, and then breathed a sigh of relief.

"What happened? What's wrong?" Tristan asked. Tristan was glowing with embarrassment as he pushed the thoughts he had just enjoyed into the back of his mind. Boris looked haggard.

"It's nothing. It's just a dream," he said.

"That's not like any dream I've ever had," Tristan said.

"No...but it doesn't mean anything. It's just...it's just something I have to deal with."

"What was the dream about?" Tristan asked. He was standing above Boris and his hands were still upon Boris' shoulders after shaking him awake. Boris tilted his head up and a strange look came upon his face, a look that Tristan couldn't quite decipher. Boris turned his gaze away and shook his head.

"You wouldn't understand. I don't want to talk about it."

"Why? Because I'm a human?" Tristan said bitterly. "Try me. Is it the first time you've had this dream?"

Boris pressed his lips together. "No."

"Then maybe it's something you should talk about."

"Talking about it won't help. Nothing will help. I..." Boris's expression flickered for a moment and then he looked directly at Tristan. "You work closely with Byron. He said that he might be able to help me learn about different talents and things that may have been forgotten in the past. Do you know anything about seers?"

Tristan tensed and licked his lips. Such a topic was not one that should be explored lightly and he wasn't sure if Byron would want him talking to Boris about it given that Tristan couldn't teach Boris as well as Byron could have. But Tristan couldn't ignore the look of fear in Boris' eyes. It was primal terror, and he wasn't about to deny himself the chance to be there for Boris.

But there was something he wanted in return.

"I know a little bit about it, although not as much as Byron," Tristan began.

"I don't care," Boris said desperately. "I just need to know *something*. I need to know that I'm not going crazy."

"Okay, but if I tell you what I know can you do a little favor for me in return? Can you take me to look at the Chalice of Sinterbaum when we get back to Lycanthia?"

"Of course," Boris said without hesitation. Tristan felt a little guilty for taking advantage of Boris' ignorance, but he was so close to what he had always wanted that he couldn't let the opportunity slip now.

"Okay…I don't know too much, but I know that it was a very powerful talent and the seers were revered. It is a skill that has been lost. As far as I know there had to be some very unique circumstances surrounding their births, circumstances that are difficult to recreate, although I do not know what these circumstances are exactly. I believe that over time the seers ended up being reviled as well as revered. People didn't like hearing about their deaths. Most of the visions were of destruction. There are writings where many believed that having visions of the future was a curse, because the only certainty was death, and their lives became defined by this. Do you...do you think you are a seer?" Tristan asked tentatively. "What do you see in your dream?"

Boris looked away and his voice was heavy with emotion. When he spoke, it was as though he was reliving a trauma.

"I'm in a field. The moon is red. It feels like everything is burning. I'm on my knees. Sometimes I'm a wolf, other times I'm not, but I'm surrounded by them. They're all chained and in pain, unable to move. Those that are alive anyway. The others are dying. I don't know what kills them. Then there's someone else, someone standing above me. They have their hand on my shoulder. I look up at them and I can't quite make out their faces but I'm filled with the sense that everything is going to be okay. But how can it be when all the wolves are dying? Do you think that could be a vision of the future? I've had these dreams so often. I don't know if I can dream of anything else anymore. It gets to the point where I'm afraid to close my eyes at night. I don't...I just want them all to go away," he said.

Tristan was silent for a few moments. He had a grave look on his face.

"I would have to check the books. Some seers did document their visions. I was always curious about them, wondering why they had never been taken more seriously. You'd be better asking Byron about them as well, but if you want an answer right here and now then yes...they certainly sound similar to things I have read and the fact that they repeat over and over again...but I don't understand. There hasn't been a seer for a long, long time. Why would you have this ability?" Tristan asked more as a general wondering than an actual question. Boris looked uncomfortable and answered brusquely.

"I don't know," he spat, which aroused Tristan's suspicions. Byron had always taught him to look at matters more deeply and to always observe people's behavior. There was something else going on here…Tristan was sure of it. But, for the time being at least, he didn't press any further. There was still much he didn't know about the prince and he didn't want to jeopardize all the goodwill he had earned. So, he stepped back and returned to his seat, falling into silence. The prince looked away, seeming to be happy to fall into his own world. Tristan tried not to gaze at the prince, but his heart was a mixture of powerful emotions. If Boris truly was a seer this could mean so much…Byron would be pleased.

Chapter Seven

Boris felt embarrassed about showing such vulnerability in front of Tristan, this man he barely knew. And yet there was something about Tristan that was familiar. The dream had confirmed it. The man standing over Boris was just like Tristan when he had awoken the prince from the dream. But did that mean Tristan was a part of his future? The warm feeling of security and safety he had from the man in the dream extended to reality. The rest of the dream was filled with terror though, and Boris didn't know how he was going to cope if he was a seer. If this was the future then it was a very bad one, and he had to share it with someone as soon as possible. At least he had Byron now. Byron seemed to know what he was talking about. It would all be cleared up, as soon as they made it back to Lycanthia.

For the rest of the flight Boris remained quiet, and Tristan respected that. Tristan's tale of his childhood had moved Boris. As soon as they made it to America they went to their hotel, where they were given separate rooms next to each other, but then made a point to go to Triss' store. They were only staying a few days, so it wasn't a long trip, and already Boris was eager to return home.

The streets of America were almost as familiar to him as those of Lycanthia as they trigged a childhood memory. He directed a car to the store. Tristan had earnestly asked to join him, and Boris had agreed, if somewhat reluctantly. Although, for the time being he didn't mind the company.

Being surrounded by another city was a relief for Boris. Here, he could forget about his dreams and all the grim portents of the future. Lycanthia was a place forgotten by the rest of the world. It was a place where magic still reigned and where people were enchanted by various things. In America everything was different. It was brighter, bigger, and bolder. The buildings were more ostentatious and everyone walked around with purpose, usually wedded to some item of technology, and they were usually only ever concerned with their own lives as well. Here he didn't have to worry about being a prince. Nobody paid any attention to him, and there was something freeing about that.

He knew his father had experienced something similar when he had first come to these shores so many years ago, when the prince of Lycanthia had met a young man working in an antique store. Their lives had become entwined and were instantly inseparable. It hadn't failed to occur to him that there were some parallels between their story and his own since Tristan had joined him, but he wasn't going to pay much attention to that. He was still adamant that he didn't need anyone, even though he couldn't deny the strange longing in his heart, and the profound sense of wellbeing he felt when he was with Tristan.

"Is your home like this too?" Boris asked Tristan.

"Some of the cities are, but Byron and I live out in the country where it's quiet. It's a lot like Lycanthia. We have a cottage in the middle of nowhere. There's not another soul for miles. We're surrounded by fields and forests and there's just a single road that passes us by. It's perfect for us," Tristan said. It did indeed sound perfect, a place truly meant for a wolf. Boris found himself envious of Byron. The man had left Lycanthia and had managed to forge a life for himself that Boris would have loved. How freeing it would be to be able to change into a wolf whenever he wanted! The only thing missing was the rest of the pack.

Thinking about them made Boris' heart fill with sorrow as the images of his dream thundered through his mind again. He was glad to see the antique store ahead. He quickened his pace, eager to see Triss, and burst through the door. Tristan was a few paces behind. Triss was standing behind the counter and smiled when she looked up and saw that Boris had arrived. She briskly walked from behind the counter and embraced him tightly. Her flaming red hair was still as vivid as ever, and her green eyes shone with happiness. She smelled of lilacs and as Boris inhaled her aroma he felt immediately at peace.

"Boris, I'm so happy you made it. It's been too long," Triss said kindly. The world had been good to her. She retained youthful beauty and a happy outlook on life. The store reflected her really; it was open and bright, with all the items and trinkets waiting to be picked up and explored. She had a natural inquisitiveness that meant there was a vast array of items on display, ordered in no particular way. "And you've brought a friend?" Triss added when she saw Tristan.

Tristan noticed that he had been noticed and bowed as he had before the king. Triss laughed and shook her head.

"You don't have to worry about all that with me," Triss said, "We're not in a castle now."

Tristan looked confused. Boris explained who he was, and then suggested that Tristan should go and explore the store to see if there was anything that he found interesting. "Tristan has been on many adventures around the world and he likes to look at different artifacts," Boris said.

"A man after my own heart," Triss said with a wide smile. She gestured to her store with an outstretched hand. "Well please, have a good look at what I have to offer. I like to think that everything in the store is just waiting for the right person to come along and snatch it up. If you don't mind, I'd like to spend a few moments catching up with my son."

Triss gave Boris a knowing smile as she linked arms with him and led him to the rear of the store, where they would be out of earshot.

"I assume he doesn't know about the details of your parentage?" Triss asked.

"You'd be right, although he is aware of my other secret."

"I see," Triss inclined her head. "I take it all is well in Lycanthia?"

Boris looked uneasy, and Triss' body language changed. Her head tilted to one side and her features became softer. "What's wrong?" she asked without him having to reply. Even though they were not biologically related he and Triss still shared a bond, and it was one that was strong even though they saw each other irregularly.

"I've been having a tough time lately. I know I'm not the prince I should be, or the man I should be. I'm afraid that I've offended Dad because all I want is to be a wolf. Being a human just doesn't seem to have as much going for it. I wish that I could explain to him why I feel the way I feel because I don't want him to think that it's personal."

"You know being human isn't always a bad thing. We do have a few advantages," Triss said with a suggestive look in her eyes, but she quickly realized that Boris wasn't in a humorous mood. "I'm sure both your fathers know that you respect them and that you love them equally. It must be difficult being a child of two worlds, always feeling that you have to choose between one and the other, especially when one is so new to you. I know it's not exactly the same, but I can understand how you feel. When I was younger there were certain things expected of me when all I wanted to do was escape and explore the world. I never wanted to be a typical girl. I knew it was difficult on my father. I wasn't what he wanted from a daughter, and it was only fortune that led to me marrying the prince and giving father everything he wanted. If I hadn't managed to strike that bargain, I know I would have left Lycanthia anyway and he would have been heartbroken. It's not cruel of us to do these things; we have to be true to the desires that exist within our hearts and we can only ever be beholden to our own happiness."

"But that's not true for me. I am a prince."

"And I am a Queen," Triss said with a light chuckle. "We can make our own rules to our life. Your fathers did," she said, placing a hand on Boris' shoulder. "Now then, tell me what else is troubling you. I can tell that something is weighing deeply on your mind."

Triss was perhaps the one person who Boris didn't mind talking about his dreams with. She was removed from Lycanthia and the world of the wolves, which meant she was completely objective and could offer advice without being influenced by anything else. Boris told her what he had dreamed. Triss looked pensive. She placed a calming hand against his cheek and the effort was soothing.

"Have you told anyone about this?"

"No," Boris said, "only Tristan because I had a nightmare on the plane."

"Boris, you know that you need to talk to somebody about this. This is serious. They can help you. You know they'd want to know. Why have you been so reticent to tell them?"

"Because I'm scared," he said honestly.

"I know," Triss said, breathing sharply. "I'm sure it's very scary, but part of that is because you're going through this alone. I think it's good that you told Tristan at least, but you must speak to your fathers and to your grandmother. They'll be able to help you more than anyone else can. Maybe you're putting too much pressure on yourself. Maybe the wolves that are chained in your dream are your fears that if you accept your human side, you'll have to sacrifice that part of yourself."

"But I know that's not true," Boris said.

"Sometimes we can know something is true and yet it still bothers us. I want you to promise me that as soon as you get back home, you'll go and tell someone about this, okay?"

"Okay," Boris said reluctantly. Triss patted his cheek and then took her hand away.

"Good, that's what I like to hear. I may not be a wolf, but I'm still pretty wise in these matters. Now, tell me, how are Eric and Shane?"

"They're very well," Boris said, and proceeded to tell her about the latest happenings in Lycanthia. Triss updated him about the things that were happening in her life as well. She traveled as much as she could, but also enjoyed various random people coming into the store.

"It's funny, but people still don't know the truth," Boris said. "They still wonder what happened between you and the king."

"And let's hope things stay that way. I never quite agreed with your grandmother's fondness for secrecy, but in this instance, I think it's warranted. I'm not sure the world is ready for this particular truth. I'm sure that a lot of them think I'm a very bad mother and an ungrateful queen as well," Triss said. Boris looked away uncomfortable and mumbled something awkward, but Triss waved a hand away. "Good thing that I never particularly cared for what other people think. So, you're about the age now when you have to start thinking about the future I suppose. Has there been any talk about it?"

"A little," Boris said, and stiffened with tension, a fact that didn't go unnoticed by Triss. "But I don't want to talk about that. Nothing is going to happen. I don't need anyone else." He sounded bullish, and Triss enjoyed a little smirk.

"I see, well that's very independent of you. But Boris, did you ever think that perhaps someone might need you?" The blank look on his face answered her question. "I wouldn't go dismissing this whole area of life just yet. After all, you've only just begun discovering your wolf side and you've seen what delights it can offer. This part is one of the more rewarding sides of humanity, and I don't think you should dismiss your human side until you try it for yourself."

Boris looked unsure of himself and indeed a little flustered. To Triss, all of these things came quite naturally, and she had a cavalier attitude about discussing them, but Boris was the opposite. "I think your friend is waiting for us," Triss said, looking over Boris' shoulder. Boris turned around to see Tristan standing there, glancing toward them.

"He's not my friend," Boris said, "he's just my tutor's assistant."

***

Despite saying this, Boris and Tristan did spend a lot of time together on their trip. They stayed in the store for a while. Boris was happy to help out Triss as they talked more about life in general and he got updates on some of her recent vacations. Triss was all too happy to share tales of the places she had seen and the people she had encountered, and Tristan shared some stories of his own as well. It turned out that he and Triss had been to some similar areas of the world and they bonded over these, which made Boris feel left out. He had always been proud of his devotion to his country and never felt as though he needed to leave it to have an enriching life, but as he sat there listening to Triss and Tristan he couldn't help but feel as though he was missing out on a whole world. Tristan came alive in a way that Boris hadn't seen him do so yet, and for the first time Boris saw him truly enthused about a subject. He spoke with passion and knowledge and injected his stories with humor. He and Triss got on well, and Boris wondered why he could never get on that well with people he had just met.

There was more than one occasion when Boris found Tristan gazing at him, and Boris returned the gesture. There was something about Tristan that he found intriguing, and when it came to the end of the night Boris found that he didn't want it to end. They stood outside their rooms and smiled awkwardly at each other, until Boris invited Tristan in under the guise of not being tired yet.

Tristan accepted without hesitation.

Chapter Eight

Tristan couldn't believe what he had heard earlier. As soon as they had departed from the plane Tristan had taken his daily elixir that helped heighten his senses. He had been awed by Triss' store, but even more by what he had overhead. He hadn't intended to eavesdrop. It had happened entirely by accident, all because Triss and Boris hadn't been able to believe that he was able to hear their conversation. Byron would be intrigued by the truth, and what Tristan had heard went some way to explaining why Boris was so special. Triss wasn't his mother at all; he was the product of two men!

Such a thing was not unheard of, but it was rare, and it would go some way to explaining why he had the abilities of a seer. Tristan had only read about such things, and even when reading about them they had seemed so astonishing that he thought there must have been some mistranslation along the way. He was in the presence of a living miracle.

He had to hold his tongue though. All through dinner he was able to lose himself in the company of Triss, who made for very engaging conversation. She may not have wanted to be a Queen, but she acted in a very regal manner. She was polite, inquisitive, and she made sure that there was not a dull moment during the entire evening. However, Tristan had noticed that Boris was subdued, so when they were finally alone (and how Tristan had prayed for Boris to ask him into his hotel realm and to push back the end of the evening) Tristan decided to ask him about it.

"You seemed a little off tonight. Is everything alright, or are you still dwelling on your dream?" Tristan asked. The room had a comfortable glow. The night was warm enough for a window to be open, through which a cool breeze drifted. Outside the city glittered as brightly as the night sky did in Lycanthia.

"I'm fine," Boris said as he sat on one end of the couch. Tristan took the other end. "It's just that when I listen to you and Triss talk about all the places you've seen, well, it makes me feel as though I've never lived at all. And it's strange because in my heart I know I will never need anything more than Lycanthia, but it is such a small country and the world is so big. I suppose it's just humbling when I know that I will never get to experience it all."

"I have the same feeling every time I hear talk of wolves," Tristan admitted.

"You do?"

Tristan nodded. "Ever since I discovered it was a possibility it was all I wanted to be. I used to ask my parents why I couldn't be a wolf. I didn't understand that it was not a matter of choice or perseverance. I would have given anything to be like you. Tell me, what is it like for you to turn into a wolf?" he asked.

Boris hung his head and smiled. "It's like nothing I've ever experienced before. There's a rush of blood and this intoxicating feeling that comes over me. The world gets brighter and I feel so powerful. I feel like there's nothing I can't do, and when I'm running along beside my pack, I know that we're a force of nature. There's nothing that can stand in our way. I feel free. I feel complete. I feel that I'm where I belong. And I suppose that I can't believe there was ever a time when I couldn't change into a wolf."

"It sounds amazing," Tristan said. "I wish I could experience it myself. I've never felt like that. All my life I've felt as though there's something different about me, as though I'm supposed to be special but I don't know how. It feels like there's something beyond my reach and all I need to do is grasp it, but I have no idea where to look or how to find it. I don't know…I guess I don't make much sense," he added with a smile, looking sheepish.

"No, it's okay. I've often felt like I don't belong, at least in the human world. I guess that's what comes with being a wolf. I'm just glad I live in a time when the pack can run together."

"Yes, Byron often speaks with regret that the Queen made wolves go into isolation and prided secrecy above everything else. He says that a lot of knowledge was lost."

"That's why I want him as a teacher. I think he can teach me great things, especially if he can tell me more about this dream."

"What are you going to do if it turns out you are a seer?" Tristan asked.

"I suppose I'll try and stop whatever is happening in my dream. I don't want the wolves to die. I don't want anyone to die. Is there anything else you know about seers? Anything you can tell me?"

Tristan searched his mind. "There is one thing, although I'm not sure you really want to hear it."

"No, please, tell me. I need to know everything."

"I told you before that the seers weren't the most popular people around. The thing with their visions is that they're not reliable. You don't know what leads to the vision. The very thing you do to avoid it might be the thing that leads to that outcome. Byron will be able to tell you more, but I would suggest that you go carefully."

"Do you think I should avoid it entirely then?"

"I'm not sure how you can, but I think it's important that you don't take it as something that will definitely happen," Tristan said. Boris looked thoughtful. He shifted his position on the couch and leaned forward. He looked pensive and rested his chin on his hand.

"It's difficult to ignore. It's in my mind all the time, even when I'm not sleeping. At first, I hoped to just push it away, but then it came back. Now every time it comes to me in my sleep it feels stronger and more powerful. I'm not sure I can ignore it even if I wanted to. If there's a chance that this could mean the end of the wolves, I have to do everything I can do stop it. I can't just stand by and do nothing." He rose in a flurry of anguish and strode toward the window, looking out upon the city.

"Look at this place," Boris said, stretching out a hand as though he was encompassing the entire city. "None of them down there know anything about Lycanthia or care about my people. We don't matter to them. How did the world get like this, where the wolves are an endangered species? Do any of them get troubled by these haunted dreams? I doubt it, and I'm expected to put on a brave face and pretend to be a prince, to hide the wolves in plain sight? It doesn't seem fair."

"No, it doesn't," Tristan said. "The wolves shouldn't have to hide, nor should you."

"All my life I have been told to hide behind my human face. I have been told to suppress my wolfish instincts, even though I'm then told that I need to be proud of both parts of my heritage. Why should I be proud that I'm a human when they have done nothing except spread themselves across the planet in one endless plague? They don't have any special abilities. They haven't been blessed by the moon! They're just normal, ordinary. Why should I be ashamed of wanting to be a wolf? Why should I have to limit myself like this?"

"You shouldn't," Tristan said. Boris turned. His eyes flashed wildly and there was an irresistible energy emanating from his body. Tristan was caught up in his flurry of emotion. It all made sense, every word of it. Tristan knew the anguish well, but at least Boris had a way to free himself of his weak flesh. He could break free from the prison that held him, while Tristan could only fool himself into thinking he was better with the elixirs and potions that had been specially made for him.

"You should let yourself be free, as often as you like. You should shift now Boris. Howl to the mood and declare that you are a creature of the night. You are a superior specimen and you deserve to be worshiped, not consigned to the darkness. Change now Boris. Shift into the animal you were always meant to be. Don't force yourself to be locked into your flesh. Show me the animal inside. Show me who you really are!" Tristan's voice grew with intensity as he spoke. He was almost trembling. His eyes met with Boris and for a moment there was a flicker of doubt in the prince's eyes, but within a flash of a moment that doubt vanished.

Tristan's heart fluttered with excitement as he watched Boris shift. The air seemed to shimmer around him as the magic took hold. His clothes faded and his flesh rippled as sleek fur grew from the pores, covering his body. He fell to his legs and his body stretched out, his face became longer and his eyes were beady, but the essence of the soul was still visible inside his eyes. He was every bit as beautiful as a wolf as he was as a man, and as soon as he was in his natural form he tilted his neck back and let out a bestial howl, one that made Tristan's body tingle with excitement. His flesh prickled and breath caught in his throat. There was something different about seeing Boris shift than there was when he saw Byron do the same thing. There was a different energy in the air.

Tristan walked up to Boris and tentatively reached out a hand. Boris dipped his head, allowing Tristan to place his palm on Boris' head. The fur was soft, which was somewhat surprising given that the wolf was a predator, with sharp teeth and deadly claws. Tristan's fingers ran through the fur and he let out a soft moan. He brought his hand around the wolf's face, running under his chin, feeling the warm breath against his hands. To be in such close proximity with a wolf made Tristan's heart thunder. His eyes filled with tears as it was so beautiful and bittersweet; painful because he knew he couldn't experience the same thing himself.

"You're amazing," Tristan said, and then laughed with joy as he watched Boris bound around the room, deftly jumping over the couch and then wriggling under the coffee table. He chased his tail and was like a blur as he sped around the room, before landing on the bed, pink tongue lolling out, panting. Tristan gazed at him with great ardor, but something strange happened to Boris. He was standing on the bed, and opposite him was a mirror hanging on the wall. As he moved around, he caught sight of his reflection and he stopped, hanging his head. The air shimmered as the magic was released and Boris returned to his original form, sitting on the bed with slumped shoulders.

Tristan walked up to him and joined him on the bed. Every movement was tentative as he felt a surge of heat in every part of his body, and he wasn't sure that Boris felt the same thing. He looked into the mirror. When he saw the two of them sitting there, he was overwhelmed with how right it seemed. Tristan had never dealt with these feelings before, but when they were so strong inside him, he couldn't believe that Boris wasn't feeling the same thing. They were feeding off each other.

"What's wrong?" Tristan asked.

"What if I can't help them? What if they're all going to die and I can't do anything to stop it? It's bad enough having these dreams, but at least I can delude myself into thinking I can do something to stop it. But what if I'm lying to myself?"

"I don't know about these seers of the past, but I know you. I know you won't let anything happen to them. You care too much. You're going to lead them one day, just like the King. With mine and Byron's help we'll be able to get to the bottom of this prophecy. I promise you that. We'll figure out what it means, and if we have to prepare for it, we will, together."

Tristan spoke with great conviction in his voice, but Boris still remained unconvinced. Tristan's heart went out to the prince. It was as though all the emotion in the world was pouring out of him and he had no idea how to handle it. The powerful sensations whirled in his mind, just as they had done on the plane. This time he didn't retreat to the restroom. This time he stayed with Boris.

He moved closer to the prince. First, he placed a hand surreptitiously on the prince's back and then leaned in, breathing in the prince's musky scent. Tristan whispered that everything was going to be okay as he brought his face in closer and closer, until his lips brushed against the prince's. It happened so quickly that the prince was taken off guard. As soon as their lips touched, he backed away, but Tristan quickly caught Boris' head in his hands, cupping it.

"It's okay, you don't have to be afraid. I know you Boris. I know everything and it's okay," Tristan said. His words were breathless and they soon drifted into the air as he pressed his lips against Boris' again, this time more firmly. There was a moment of resistance and a muffled protest, but that vanished as Boris yielded to the kiss. Tristan felt the sweet feeling of pleasure run through his body as he felt the softness of Boris' lips and the heat of the breath coming onto him. His hands roamed around Boris' back, feeling the sinews of his back and the broad muscles that stretched underneath his taut skin. Their lips parted and their tongues danced together. The air simmered with heat everything came naturally to the men. Long dormant feelings were freed and they ran rampant. Their hands clawed at clothes and nailed dragged down their skin. Tristan was filled with the controllable urge to give everything he had. He buried himself in the crook of Boris' neck, breathing in the hot scent. His other hand roamed across Boris' chest, feeling the soft hair, diving down to the dark depths of Boris' body.

Both men were letting their instincts guide them. They fell on the bed, their bodies entwined like vines. They groaned and grunted as they pulled their clothes away and exposed their flesh. Boris' body was unexplored territory. Tristan was the eager conqueror, his hands were like ships traversing the seas, his tongue and lips darted around the ocean of flesh and were scorched by the ravaging heat. A song of lust thrummed through his body, and his mind became chaotic. Boris tilted his body back and offered the hollow of his throat, which Tristan took with glee. His weight rested on Boris' frame and he could feel the swell of arousal. Tristan's eager hand dived down and brushed against the taut skin. Tristan's hands danced over the flesh and he grinned, excited by the fact that from this skin came fur.

A delirious, exhilarating feeling surged through him as his hand ran down Boris' inner thigh and squeezed the powerful muscle. He was so close to the burning masculinity that he twitched and almost doubled over. At first, he thought of teasing Boris, until he realized that he couldn't help himself. As soon as he had his hand wrapped around the tight skin, he knew what he needed to do. He let his natural instincts guide him, as well as the fervent moans rushing from Boris' mouth. Tristan stroked and teased, ran his thumb over the mushroom tip and moaned in delight as he felt Boris harden.

While Tristan was doing this Boris mirrored his movements. His hand reached down and Tristan groaned with harsh, ardent sounds as his own erection was taken into hand. The two men pleasured each other, stroking and squeezing until they could barely take anymore. They shifted their bodies. Their flesh glistened with aroused sweat and the slickness swept against each other as they turned their bodies around, both wanting to devour each other. They began to pleasure each other with their mouths. Warm saliva dripped down. Tristan's eyes fluttered open and in the murky darkness he could see Boris' warm lips wrapped around his manhood. The sight was so intense that Tristan almost lost consciousness.

But there was no way he was going to faint when so many blissful and bright emotions were crashing through his body. Tristan lost all sense of time and space as he buried himself in the act of making love to Boris' body. The two young men were in the prime of life and their bodies were ready for this. It was as though the first kiss between them had opened the floodgates to deep desires that had been hidden inside. Because of their respective natures they had indulged or explored these desires before. It had been a hidden realm for them both, and only together could they peel back the layers of the world and face these most primal feelings.

For Tristan it was as though some other force had possessed him. He was aware of everything happening in his body, but it was moving so quickly, so instinctively that it was faster than his thoughts. The whole thing was a blur and then suddenly, he was turned and twisted around. Boris' strong hands were on him, guiding him, his fingers digging into the supple flesh. Their lips brushed together and their breath mingled as one. The rush of air was calming and pleasing. Tristan found his body bent as he got on two knees. His elbows rested against the soft surface of the bed. As he tilted his head up, he looked out to the night sky, out to paradise.

Boris's hands were all over him, roaming across his chest, feeling his erection, even running over his mouth. His fingers slid in between his lips and they were covered with saliva, which made it all the more pleasing when Boris started to play with Tristan's most intimate area. It was something he had never experienced before, something he had never even thought of before, but it opened a whole new world of pleasure. Vibrant ripples careened through his body and seemed to grow in strength with every passing moment. His head bowed and his eyelids clamped shut. He grabbed a fistful of the bed sheets as he tried to process the sensations that ran through his body.

And then there was something else. Something big. Something that made his mouth form an 'O' and for silent moans to come out in choking breaths. Every inch of his body trembled. Shuddering breaths made his heart flutter as he felt Boris ease inside him. The pain was exquisite and he could feel his eyes filling with water as the intensity was almost too much to bear, but it quickly gave way to the most unbelievable pleasure. It was as though a bright glow flashed in his mind and he was bathed in the most glorious, ethereal light. He twisted his neck around and was greeted with the sight of Boris' muscular body slamming against him. The pleasing angles were coated in sweat. Boris' head was flung back in ecstasy and his hands were upon Tristan's hips, holding him steady and tight. The heat rose between them and the air simmered. Tristan cried out in pleasure.

He could feel something growing inside him, something simmering and bubbling with the full force of a supernova. It was as though another force had been given life inside him. It was writhing and churning and begging to break free. His manhood throbbed with a need to release everything that was burning inside. His throat was raw with the fevered moans. Boris was so deep inside him he was reaching places that Tristan had never known existed, and then it was as though he had hit a wall. The feelings bubbled inside him. Tristan had tried to hold them off for as long as possible, but in the end, the force had been irresistible and it had all flowed out in one burst. He doubled over as he came, and his entire body tensed. This meant that it did more for Boris. The tightened orifice gave Boris another sensation and expedited the orgasm, forcing it to rush out. A wide, satisfied smile broke out on Tristan's face as he let the warmth settle into him. It flowed like a warm river and felt luxurious. His mind simmered as he sank down and melted into a puddle on the bed. Boris came up behind him and wrapped his arms around him, kissing him on the nape of the neck.

Tristan's body was alive with the prince's heat. He hadn't realized until that moment how badly he had needed this comfort until now. Being held by him was to be protected from all the ills of the world. It was as though nothing could hurt him again, as though nothing could ever make him unhappy. He closed his eyes and thought of nothing but the prince, pushing away the feelings of guilt he felt, for he would have to betray the prince's confidence to obey Byron.

A dark shadow obscured his heart and he shifted uncomfortably. It had seemed such a simple request when Byron had first made it, but now it seemed wrong. His feelings for the prince were genuine, but he could never break his loyalty to Byron. The man was akin to his own father, had raised him and given him shelter when he had lost everything. Tristan would enjoy everything this tryst with the prince could bring him, but in the end his first loyalty was with Byron the Black Wolf.

Chapter Nine

Boris slumped onto the pillow. His mind and body were alive with all kinds of different sensations. He never knew that anything could be so primal and joyous, and he started to understand about some of the advantages of human life. Being in the throes of passion was akin to living as a wolf. The world became brighter and greater. His senses were heightened and everything became vivid. It was so easy to lose himself in the miasma of his passion, and so simple to get confused by the thoughts and emotions that raged within his mind.

What did this mean?

Was this love, or was it something else? Could there be anything else? He rested his head against the nape of Tristan's neck and closed his eyes, listening to the rhythm of Tristan's breathing. His hands were wrapped around the man's chest, and their bodies were pressed against each other. Boris could feel the frantic beating of Tristan's heart against the palm of his hand, and the slick sheen of sweat upon his body. He breathed deeply and fell asleep, being lulled by the presence of this man.

When Boris woke, he was stunned to find that he had enjoyed a completely restful sleep He hadn't twisted and turned, nor had he experienced the dream again. Tristan was on the other side of the bed. Boris pulled at his hand and rolled him over. Tristan's eyes cracked open, awake as the morning sun poured in through the wide windows. Boris let his fingers entwine with Tristan's and they smiled at each other. There was so much that was uncertain, so much that Boris did not know. It was unexplored territory for him.

He decided to be honest.

"That was the best night's sleep I've had in ages," he said.

"Mine too. I have to admit that I didn't expect that to happen on this trip."

"You hoped it would though, didn't you?" Boris asked, afraid that he was a little too forthright. Tristan averted his gaze and his cheeks flushed, embarrassed.

"How did you know?"

"Call it wolfish instinct. I noticed the way you were looking at me. I wasn't sure how to deal with it at first. All my life I've been proud of the fact that I've never needed anyone before, but now I'm starting to realize that sometimes it's not about what I need, it's about what I want. That used to be being alone, but now I'm not so sure. I haven't really met anyone like you. I've never been able to talk about this stuff with anyone before."

"That's what I'm here for," Tristan said. He let his hand linger across Boris' face. His long fingers caressed Boris' cheek and Boris enjoyed the relaxing sensation. He took deep breaths and murmured his satisfaction. Tristan pressed his lips lightly against Boris' and the two of them drowned in another tight embrace again, before they spent the rest of the day together exploring the city.

***

Boris was in high spirits when he said goodbye to Triss. The trip was a brief one, as always, but a lot had happened. It had afforded him the chance to become close with Tristan and he was eager to return to Lycanthia to see where it was going to lead. Triss gave him a knowing smile and told him to be careful, for matters of the heart could always lead him into trouble.

"I'm confident of handling anything," Boris said.

But he was always wary of making anything public, so before they landed back in Lycanthia he spoke to Tristan.

"I know this probably isn't what you want to hear, but do you mind if we keep what happened between us for now? It's just that as a prince I'm under a lot of scrutiny anyway and so much of my life is public. I'd quite like there to be something that's just for me for a change, at least for a little while, until we figure out what this all means."

"Of course, but you'll still take me to see the Chalice of Sinterbaum, won't you?" Tristan said. Boris wasn't entirely sure why Tristan was so intent on seeing some old chalice, but he nodded away, not seeing any harm in it. He was pleased to see the landscape of Lycanthia appear on the horizon. He and Tristan exchanged some heated kisses before they landed, and then they smiled shyly at each other. Keeping their relationship a secret added an extra layer of excitement to it as well, and while Boris didn't want that to remain true for too long, he was at least glad that it gave him some time to adjust to the new circumstances and figure out what was going on in his mind.

The most important thing was figuring out this vision, but at least with Tristan's calming presence, he might be able to have some breathing space.

***

As soon as he returned home his parents were eager to hear about his trip and he gave them all the details.

95

"It was actually a good suggestion," Boris said. "I think that having a few days away was good to clear my head, and Mother always has some words of wisdom," he said. He was still afraid to tell them about the dream. He wanted to tell Byron first, since Byron seemed to know more about the history of the wolves, so at the first opportunity he went to the man who was to be his teacher.

During their absence, Byron had made himself quite at home in one of the rooms in the upper tower of the castle. The view was quite wonderful from the balcony. Tall and wide bookshelves had been carried up the stairs and installed in the room. Boris didn't envy the people who had to carry them up the stairs, along with all the books. Some of them looked very old and while he wasn't ordinarily a studious person, the age of the books was alluring. Tristan stood beside Byron and smiled. A secret glance was shared between the two boys and Boris blushed. He didn't think Byron suspected anything.

"Ah good, you're here early. I wasn't expecting to start until tomorrow given you have just returned from your trip, but I always appreciate enthusiasm in my students. Please, take a seat," he gestured to a single seat in the room. Boris took it and stretched his hands along the desk, eager to begin his education. Byron started to talk about the curriculum he envisioned for Boris and gave the student a brief overview of what he expected. Such a thing was not what Boris wanted. He had spent so long yearning to uncover more about the nature of the wolves, the history of Lycanthia, and now, after speaking with Tristan, he knew that Byron might help him unlock the secrets of his own mind as well.

"I was hoping we might take a somewhat different path," Boris said, interrupting Byron. Byron pursed his lips and clasped his hands behind his back. It was evident that he was holding back his tongue, wary of scolding the prince in case word should spread back to the King. If he did that Byron's time in the castle might be short. Boris knew that's what he was thinking anyway. It wasn't true; Eric wasn't that petty, but the thought allowed Boris and advantage and he pressed it.

"And what path would that be? It's not usual for the student to dictate terms to the teacher," Byron said in a terse voice. His eyes narrowed slightly, and his features looked more angular than usual.

"I think you know what I want to learn about. You mentioned it the first night we met. In fact, that's the entire reason why I pleaded with my father to allow you to teach me. If you're going to take your time in getting to my most desired subject, then my appraisal of you may not be as complimentary as it might otherwise be," Boris said. Byron shifted uncomfortably and sighed heavily at the prince's allusion. His eyes closed. Boris knew that he had irked the teacher, but he didn't care, as long as he got what he wanted.

"I suppose you are hinting at the dream? Yes, Tristan did mention that you were intrigued by the nature of the seers." A gleam shimmered across Byron's eyes. "It is a long, lost art, one that was most rare and precious. Personally, I think it is something that we could use a little more of. Who wouldn't wish to know the future? It would allow us to prepare for anything..." he paced in front of Boris. The prince glanced over at Tristan, a little annoyed that Tristan had told Byron something of their trip. He wondered what else Tristan had told him.

"It is not a subject that is easy to discuss," Byron said. "There are few people who understand the nuances, and we are going to have to work together very diligently to get the truth of the matter. Such answers are going to be buried in the past and we are going to have to dig with all the strength we can muster," Byron brought one of his hands around to the front of his body and clenched it in a fist. "But I have no doubt we can get to the bottom of this." His gaze had been fixed on a far point in the room, but now it fell upon Boris and focused on him in a heavy glare.

"However," Byron continued, "it is a matter of utmost secrecy. There are people who would think prying into such matters is dangerous. Seers were often treated with suspicion and mistrust. It pains me to say that such attitudes still prevail today. Until we find some solid proof about all of this, we must keep it between us. We shall merely be two scholars who are investigating and studying a long-forgotten phenomenon." He offered a sly smile. "Is that agreeable to you my prince?"

Boris considered the matter a moment. Triss had urged him to share the truth with his family, but he hadn't yet and nothing bad had happened. It seemed prudent to keep it that way until he had something substantial to tell them. After all, at the moment, the only thing he was suffering from was a bad dream and that didn't amount to much. He needed to know more before he could go to his family and worry them.

"I agree," Boris said, glancing toward Tristan before he committed to the promise.

"Splendid," Byron said, now clasping his hands together in front of him. "I'm sure we shall learn a lot. But I shall need to know more about your desire to learn about the seers and what dreams plague your mind. I am going to need you to be honest Boris. Please, leave nothing out. The dreams of seers can often be chaotic and surreal. Every small detail is important. If you truly are a seer then I must have an accurate picture of the images in your mind. Communicate to me what you have seen; only then can I help you."

Boris took a deep breath and then told him everything he had told Tristan. It was somehow easier to talk about now that he had shared it with someone else, although he was certain that a great majority of this feeling was because Tristan was in the room. It was just a shame that he couldn't reach out to Tristan for comfort, strength, and support. As exciting as the clandestine nature of their romance would be, Boris also quickly realized that it was going to be frustrating.

His voice grew haggard and horse as he described the images in his mind. They were so vivid and had occurred so often that he could recite every detail by heart. Breath choked and his chest tightened, as happened every time he relieved these thoughts. The most striking thing was the blood red moon. Every night he looked up at the sky and was so afraid that it would be the night when he finally saw that horrible portent come into his field of vision. The moon was beautiful when it was silver, but in his dreams, it was an ugly red welt, a throbbing sphere of doom that was waiting to crash down and wreak havoc upon his life.

By the end of his retelling, Boris was shaking and he had to hold onto his desk so tightly that his knuckles went white. He was filled with the bitter distaste of shame. It wasn't proper for a prince to be so stricken with fear, especially not a wolf prince. How he wished he could shift in that moment. As a wolf there was no fear. There was only the hunt.

Byron tapped his finger against his lips.

"That is most intriguing, and quite a stark picture. I can see why it has left you quite shaken. I am most interested in the blood moon…" he drifted off for a moment and then, with a surprising burst of speed he moved to the bookshelves and examined various books on the shelves. He pulled some off and tossed them on the floor. They landed with a thud and opened, the pages fluttering with freedom. Tristan scurried around Byron, picking up the books the black wolf so casually tossed and gathering them in his arms, dodging the falling books. Byron's dark cloak billowed behind him as he moved, but his search was fruitless.

"I'm afraid the book I'm looking for is not here. I'm certain I have read a prophecy about a blood moon before. It must be in one of the volumes that have not been transferred here yet. I will examine it later, but fear not Boris, we shall get to the bottom of this dream, and if it is a portent of the future, we shall ensure that it does not come to pass. We wolves have to stick together after all," Byron moved away from the shelves toward Boris. He stood to the side of Boris, looming over him with one hand placed on the prince's shoulder. Boris gulped and nodded. At least he had help now. At least he had someone he could trust.

***

The lesson ended soon after that. Byron was eager to return to his home and search for this book, and he suspected that Boris wasn't of the right mental capacity to continue with the lesson after sharing his vision. Boris was relieved that things would at least progress in the manner he wanted. He would finally get to the bottom of this vision.

As soon as they were alone, Tristan came up to him and held him.

"I'm sorry that I had to tell Byron about your vision. I didn't tell him the specifics. I just made it clear that you needed his help." Tristan kissed him on the cheek and looked at him earnestly. Whatever annoyance Boris felt about the matter faded within moments.

"Don't worry about it Tristan. I understand why you told him. You were only looking out for me. I appreciate it," Boris said with a wide smile. "And I feel better for sharing it with him. I think that he can really help me. I'm looking forward to getting to the bottom of this, and the sooner the better."

"Why are you in such a rush?" Tristan asked. A grim countenance came upon Boris' face.

"Because I have no idea when this dream is going to come to pass. It might be soon for all I know. If I don't manage to understand it before it's too late, I'll never forgive myself. I can't let anything happen to the wolves Tristan, I can't."

"And you won't," Tristan took his hand and squeezed it tightly. It was funny, Boris thought, he had always felt powerful, but when Tristan was beside him and looking at him with so much adoration in his eyes he felt as though he could take on the world. He felt as powerful as he did when he was a wolf.

"Let's get out of this cramped room and do something to take our minds off all this. Just because we're back from our trip doesn't mean the fun has to end," Tristan said with a wicked gleam in his eye. Boris found it easy to get swept up in his enthusiasm.

"What did you have in mind?"

"Well…I was hoping you'd live up to your end of the bargain," Tristan said.

"I mean, I don't think seeing some old chalice is my idea of fun, but if that's what you really want to do, I'm sure it can be arranged, as long as we can go outside afterwards. I have an urge to be outside in nature today," Boris said. Tristan nodded enthusiastically and almost jumped on the spot with excitement. Boris had never seen anyone so excited about seeing an old relic before. He shook his head slightly but was glad that he could do something to make Tristan happy considering everything that Tristan had done for him. It was strange to think how quickly Tristan had come to mean so much for him when just a few days previously Boris had no idea he existed. He wondered if it was the same for his parents…the thought of romance scared him. It wasn't something he planned for and he had no idea if he could cope with it. There was so much that was uncertain, but when the thoughts became too much for him to handle, he looked up at Tristan and a calm feeling swept through him.

They made their way through the castle to the depths of the lower levels where the hallways were lit with torches and the air was cold. Recesses had been built into the walls, housing old items that had a lot of sentimental significance for the family. There were swords, spears, shields, suits of armor, gifts from other kingdoms, collections of treasure and more.

"This is heaven," Tristan said as he gazed upon it all, but there was only one thing he really wanted to see. Boris assumed that a man like Tristan would want to take his time and look at everything, but he wasn't lying when he said that he only wanted to see the chalice. Boris tried to entertain him with stories about the other artifacts. Freya had brought him down to this area of the castle many times when he was a child and had told him a lot about his history and his heritage. But Tristan didn't seem to be interested at all. Always his gaze darted toward the end of the hallway, where the chalice resided. Boris wondered if his family history paled in comparison to the other things that Tristan had discovered during his time working with Byron. Perhaps his family wasn't so special in the grand scheme of the world. It was a humbling thought, and one that Boris didn't want to dwell on.

He led Tristan to the end of the corridor, to where the chalice awaited them. Tristan's eyes widened and he gasped, then he laughed in excitement, throwing his head back. The flames of the torch flickered on his face, casting his expression in an eerie orange glow.

"I've never seen someone so excited about a chalice before," Boris said. The chalice stood upon the pedestal and looked completely normal. A few gems were embedded into its shell, and carvings had been etched into the stem, the same type of carvings that were present at the sacred ground in the forest where the gatherings took place.

"Did nobody ever tell you what this chalice is capable of?" Tristan asked.

"It's just a chalice."

"Oh no, it's more than that. This...this is freedom. This is something that can change the world." Tristan gazed at it with a greedy look in his eyes. He licked his lips and trembled with excitement. Boris furrowed his brow. There was something amiss here. What did Tristan know that he didn't? What had his family hidden from him? Tristan reached out tentatively. His hand hovered near the Chalice of Sinterbaum and then, in one swift motion as though he was swatting a fly, he thrust his hand forward and clutched the chalice. A shocked gasp escaped his lip, as though he thought that the walls of the castle were going to crumble as soon as he touched it. A smiled widened on his face as he cupped both hands around the chalice and brought it in front of him. He looked into the smooth chalice and breathed deeply, as though he was intoxicated without even drinking from it.

"Tristan, what makes this chalice so special?" Boris asked. Fear crept into his voice. A chill ran down his spine, and a breeze rushed past his ear, as though some spirit was trying to whisper a warning.

It went unheeded.

Tristan gulped and then pulled out a small vial from his pouch. A dark liquid dripped into the chalice, trickling like blood. Tristan threw the vial down. It cracked sharply.

"Tristan, what is this?" Boris asked, this time with a stern tone in his voice.

"Don't worry Boris. It's all going to be okay," Tristan said, although he did not take his eyes off the chalice. He held it with reverence and brought it inches closer to his lips. "Byron thought this was lost, but it's not."

"What does it *do*?"

"It makes wishes come true," Tristan said. And without saying another word he brought the chalice to his lips and tilted his head all the way back. He gulped freely from the chalice. Boris didn't understand what he was witnessing. He stepped forward, somehow filled with an urge to tear the chalice away and stop Tristan from doing what he was doing, but he didn't know why…and it was too late anyway. Tristan was finished. He tore the chalice away and held it in one hand. With the other he wiped his lips. They were stained black. He looked fevered as he walked up to Boris with purpose in his eyes.

"It's going to be fine Boris. Everything is going to be wonderful," he said with utter glee. He looked as though he might explode with excitement. Before Boris could ask him anything else or enquire about what had just happened Tristan had pressed his lips against Boris' in a firm kiss. It bristled with passion and Boris felt himself succumbing to the pleasure and the passion. Tristan pushed him against the wall, suddenly filled with a strength and vigor that was unusual for a human. His hands were clawing at Boris and he grunted like an animal. The chalice dropped to the stone floor with a dull thud. Boris surrendered to his desires and kissed back. The strange liquid left a strange taste on his lips, but he did not dwell on it. Soon enough their clothes were being torn away. Nothing could stop Tristan from expressing his lust, and Boris was eager to take advantage of the hidden layers of the castle.

He groaned as he felt the hardness of the stone at his back, and the hardness of Tristan pressing against him. The chalice didn't matter any longer. Nothing did, not his future, not the dream, not anything but the present. His feelings for Tristan allowed him to exist in the here and now, to focus on his feelings, just as when he was a wolf. His body was laced with fervent passion and everything became clear. He moaned with delight as Tristan's tongue danced with his. Boris let his hands roam underneath Tristan's clothes, finding the warm flesh underneath. When he breathed in, he inhaled Tristan's scent and it was intoxicating. The feelings overwhelmed him and he was glad to know they were still powerful even though they were not away from home. This *meant* something. He didn't know what yet, but he quite enjoyed not knowing. For once it was nice to look forward to the future without a sense of dread or foreboding. He let himself drown in Tristan and flung himself on the pyre of his emotions, freeing himself to do nothing but make love.